"A five-star, delicious mystery that has great characters, a good plot, and a surprise ending. If you like a good mystery with more than one suspect, then rush out to get this book, but be sure you have the time since once you start, you won't want to put it down. I give this five stars and a 'Wow Factor' of 5+. The fudge recipes included in the book all sound wonderful. A gift basket filled with the fudge from the recipes in this book, a copy of the book, some hot chocolate mix and/or coffee, and a nice mug would be a great Christmas gift."
—**Mystery Reading Nook**

"A charming and funny culinary mystery that parodies reality show competitions and is led by a sweet heroine, eccentric but likable characters, and a skillfully crafted plot that speeds toward an unpredictable conclusion. Allie stands out as a likable and engaging character. Delectable fudge recipes are interspersed throughout the novel."
—*Kings River Life Magazine*

All Fudged Up

"A sweet treat with memorable characters, a charming locale, and a satisfying mystery."
—**Barbara Allan,** author of the Trash 'n' Treasures mysteries

All Fudged Up

"A fun book with a lively plot, set in one of
America's most interesting resorts.
All this, plus fudge!"
—**JoAnna Carl,** author of the Chocoholic mysteries

"A sweet confection of a book. Charming setting,
clever protagonist, and creamy fudge—
a yummy recipe for a great read."
—**Joanna Campbell Slan,** author of the
Kiki Lowenstein Scrap-N-Craft Mysteries
and the Jane Eyre Chronicles

"Nancy Coco's *All Fudged Up* is a delightful mystery
delivering suspense and surprise in equal measure.
Her heroine, Alice McMurphy, owner of
the Historic McMurphy Hotel and Fudge
Shop (as much of a mouthful as her delicious
fudge), has a wry narrative voice that never
falters. Add that to the charm of the setting,
Michigan's famed Mackinac Island, and you have a
recipe for enjoyment. As an added bonus, mouth-
watering fudge recipes are included. A must-
read for all lovers of amateur sleuth classic
mysteries."
—**Carole Buggé,** author of *Who Killed Blanche DuBois?*
and other Claire Rawlings mysteries

HAVE YOURSELF A
FUDGY
LITTLE
CHRISTMAS

A Candy-Coated Mystery with Recipes

Nancy Coco

KENSINGTON PUBLISHING CORP.

www.kensingtonbooks.com

KENSINGTON BOOKS are published by

Kensington Publishing Corp.
119 West 40th Street
New York, NY 10018

All Kensington titles, imprints, and distributed lines are available at special quantity discounts for bulk purchases for sales promotions, premiums, fund-raising, educational, or institutional use. Special book excerpts or customized printings can also be created to fit specific needs. For details, write or phone the office of the Kensington sales manager: Kensington Publishing Corp., 119 West 40th Street, New York, NY 10018, attn: Sales Department; phone 1-800-221-2647.

First printing: November 2020

10 9 8 7 6 5 4 3 2 1

ISBN-13: 978-1-4967-2758-9
ISBN-10: 1-4967-2758-4

Printed in the United States of America

Electronic edition:

ISBN-13: 978-1-4967-2759-6 (e-book)
ISBN-10: 1-4967-2759-2 (e-book)

This book is dedicated to Papa and Grammy—
Tom and Marlene.
You will always be in our hearts.

Chapter 1

Christmastime on Mackinac Island was a dream come true with snow and horse-drawn sleighs and Victorian cottages dressed up in colored holiday lights. I planned to spend my days making holiday fudge and my nights curled up with a warm Christmassy beverage beside a crackling fire with the man I loved. That was the plan, anyway.

Why is it that these things always turn out better in my head than in real life? I guess I hadn't planned on needing to rebuild the top floor of the Historic McMurphy Hotel and Fudge Shop. I also hadn't planned on bunking in Frances's old apartment while the contractors worked, but here I was standing in the bay window of her apartment with a cup of coffee, staring out into a cold clear sky.

Frances had been a teacher for over thirty years. She worked for my grandfather as the part-time hospitality manager for the Historic McMurphy Hotel and Fudge Shop. That meant that over the years she'd gone from working the front desk to managing the reservations to managing the housekeeping staff.

Then, after my Grammy Alice died, Frances retired from teaching and came to work at the McMurphy full-time.

Luckily she stayed to work for me after my Papa Liam died last spring. I don't know what I would have done without her to support me in my first tourist season as hotel and fudge shop owner.

As I stood staring out the window at the early-morning light. Mella, my calico cat, walked around my legs and purred, while Mal, my bichonpoo puppy, tugged at the bottom of my left pajama pant leg. It was quiet in the little apartment.

You see, after marrying my new handyman, Douglas Devaney, Frances had moved out to a small house they bought together. She'd left the bed in the apartment bedroom and a small dresser along with a small couch and a wing-backed chair and a two-person dinette in the living space. It was her intention to rent out the apartment on one of those rental-home sites. But for now, she loaned it to me and my pets.

The apartment was part of a Victorian cottage that had gotten remodeled in the '60s into four apartments. This one was in the front lower right as you faced the house. Which meant Frances had a large bay window with a view of the porch and the street and sidewalk below. The center hall of the building had been turned into the hall for all of the tenants. My front door was on the right. Mrs. Gooseman's door was on the lower left and Manfred Engle's place was above me, while Mrs. Vissor lived on the top left.

Someone had decorated the front porch with

large, old-fashioned, red and green Christmas bulbs. There was a big pine wreath on the main door. Inside, the hall was strung with tiny white fairy lights. It was pretty to look at and a touch homey. But I didn't feel very much at home.

What happened? I mused. At Halloween I had an offer from Trent Jessop—the ultimate-catch bachelor whose family owned a fortune in local businesses—to spend the winter in Chicago and make fudge out of a true commercial kitchen. There had also been an offer from the very handsome and very available police officer Rex Manning. He had a nice little house just up the street with a yard for my pets to play in.

It was such a short time ago and yet, here I was in what was left of Frances's old place, sipping out of a borrowed cup, watching the snow float down in fat flakes. Alone. Mal barked at Mella and chased her up her cat tree. The cat tree held three levels with a house on the last. It was a relic of Frances's time, covered in green carpet, but Mella enjoyed it.

My cell phone rang and I saw it was Frances. "Good morning," I said. "What's up?"

"How much longer will the contractors need before we're able to have guests at the McMurphy?" she asked. "We have people who want to come in for the Santa Fun Run as well as the holiday lights contest and exhibit."

"We're waiting on inspectors," I said. "The contractor says the new roof is done and sound, except for the floating decking, which they'll put on in the spring. The apartment and office are studded and drywall goes in today if we pass inspection. Second and third floors are clean, but I can't promise the construction in the apartment won't be bothersome."

"I can let them know," Frances said. "I don't think it'll matter; these folks are regulars for the holidays. People love their traditions, you know."

"Well, send them some photos of the inside so they can see what they're coming into. If they still want to book, then let's do it. We can use the revenue."

"How's the holiday fudge production going?"

"Orders are great," I said. "I guess being in that candy cook-off on television was great promotion. Although I hear a storm is brewing that might prevent shipments' flying in and out for a few days. So I've been working around the clock today in hopes to get it out before the storm."

"I know that little kitchen is cramped," Frances said. "How are you holding up?"

"I'm making do," I said, and watched a horse-drawn sleigh wind down the street in front of me. It had jingle bells on the reins. Somewhere in the distance snowmobiles whined. "I can't use the McMurphy kitchen until all the revisions are complete and the dust settles."

"I thought the food inspector said you could use the fudge shop now," Frances was quick to point out.

"You know I don't want to do that when people know we're under construction," I said with a frown.

There was a pause. "Do you regret not taking

Trent up on his offer to use the commercial kitchen in Chicago?"

"No, no regrets. I know it would have been better for business, but I can't believe that people would want to buy Mackinac Island fudge made in Chicago. Besides, this way I can say it's all small-batch fudge." I smiled at the thought.

"Okay, then, I'll let the guests know what kind of conditions we have at the hotel. By the way, we're supposed to help with our section of the holiday lights display this afternoon. Are you still up for that? Or should Douglas and I do it?"

"I can be there," I said. "You know I like to be as involved in the community as I can."

"People will understand if you can't, you know," Frances said. "You do push yourself too hard."

"I'll be fine," I said. "Thanks, Frances." I pressed END on my phone and sipped my warm beverage as I turned back toward the kitchen. The top of the dinette table was littered with drawings and measurements for our part of the holiday display. The theme this year was "Winter Wonderland" and we were building a replica of the 1880s Main Street complete with a horse and carriage. I'd drawn up the designs and Mr. Devaney had spent the last two weeks building the frames for the lights. Frances had several feet of various holiday lights in blue, white, green, and red. This afternoon we would be putting up the frames and stringing the lights.

I had wanted to go with purple to represent the lilac festival, but getting purple lights at this late date was not going to happen, so we settled on the Victorian Christmas theme. The light displays were going up on the large lawn in front of Fort Mackinac. People would buy tickets to benefit the children's clinic and walk through all of the displays. Then they would be able to take sleighs and ride through the neighborhoods lit up for the holiday.

The displays were to be erected today and tomorrow with an evening judging contest that night at the annual Christmas tree lighting ceremony. The judging promised a purple grand-champion ribbon, a blue first-place ribbon, and a red second-place ribbon. The grand champion's display would be showcased on the Mackinac Island website and the winner would receive a thousand dollars. I sure could use the money to help pay for the repairs to the McMurphy.

I was lucky after the roof collapsed in the end of November. My father is an architect and he was able to do some renderings for me. The insurance on the McMurphy paid for most of the repairs and the historical committee okayed our permits as long as we re-created the exterior to match the original drawings.

There was a knock on my door. Mal barked and raced to the front. She turned in circles as she barked to announce whoever it was on the other side. "Coming," I said at the second knock, and I stopped a moment to peer out the peephole in my door. "Hello?" I pulled the door open but the hallway was empty. "Mrs. Gooseman? Irma?" I paused to listen while Mal raced out into the hallway and sniffed around. But no one was there. That's when I noticed a note taped to my door. I grabbed the note, picked up my pup, and went back inside. I put Mal down and she took the opportunity to chase Mella back up the cat tree. I went to the front windows to see if I could see anyone leaving, but whoever left the note was nowhere in sight.

I opened the note. It read:

Meet me at the base of the Fort Mackinac steps at noon. It's important. Tell no one.

What the heck? I looked at the note back and front. It was handwritten in beautiful block letters. But the envelope wasn't addressed. I had no idea who it was from or whether it was intended for me or for Frances.

I glanced at the clock. It was eight a.m. I still had a few hours of fudge making before noon. Maybe it was someone from the lighting exhibit committee. They were supposed to have a surprise judge. Maybe they wanted to ask me a question. I washed my hands, put on a clean apron, and started in on the remaining batches of fudge. With any luck I'd have the rest of the fudge made and packaged fresh to go out with today's mail plane. After all, Christmas fudge was in season from just after Thanksgiving until New Year's Day. High season for the fudge shop business.

I closed the kitchen door to keep my pets out of any hot-sugar happenings and went to work.

* * *

Noon came around very quickly, and I managed to package the fudge, get dressed, and make labels for the shipping store so they could take the packages to the airport. Now to make that mysterious meeting and then help with the light display. I grabbed a warm coat, hat, gloves, and boots and put Mal's winter coat on her, then her harness. We left Mella to sleep peacefully in the beam of sun that came through the window and shone on the carpet. A glance at my phone told me I was late. Mal didn't seem to be in any hurry as she stopped and did her business in a small plowed area near the sidewalk.

"Come on, Mal," I said. "We have people waiting on us." She seemed to understand my urgency and hurried off with me. It had been snowing for three weeks now and the snow was about a foot deep. The islanders kept the roads and the sidewalks cleared for tourists and locals alike. The sky was bright blue and filled with crystals as the cold started to sink into my gloves. After dropping off the boxes of fudge to be shipped, Mal and I hurried toward the base of the fort stairs. I could hear the sound of hammering and drills in the distance as the snow-covered lawn at the foot of the fort came to life with people working on their displays. Mr. Delaney had spent weeks creating our display out of plywood. The least I could do was help to string the lights. I figured I could meet whoever left the note and if they really wanted Frances, I could point out where she was. Otherwise, I was only a few yards away from our display.

I waved at Mrs. Tunisian and Mrs. Schmidt as they

worked on the display for St. Anne's. The Catholic church had won grand-champion display the last five years in a row. That meant they held a prominent location right next to the replica Indian hut. The steps to the fort were long and steep and ran up the side of the hill. There was a ticket booth at the base for when the attraction was open. The pad in front of it was shoveled and I headed toward it. But my mystery person wasn't there. I frowned and glanced around. Whoever wanted to meet me was either late or must have been impatient and left. A glance at my phone showed me I was only five minutes late, but no one was here.

I shrugged and had turned to go when Mal pulled me to the corner of the ticket booth. "What is it, girl?" I asked as she poked her nose around the corner. I looked around the corner where my dog was and saw a pair of booted feet sticking out of the snow. "Hello?"

Whoever belonged to the boots was lying face-down in the snowbank.

"Do you need some help?" I asked. Mal barked and poked the boots with her nose. I stepped into the snowbank and squatted down to shake the person in the large hooded overcoat. "Hello? Are you okay?" The person didn't respond and my heart rate sped up. I grabbed my phone and dialed 9-1-1.

"Nine-one-one. What is your emergency?" I was startled by the deep male voice on the other end.

"I'm sorry," I said because I was expecting Charlene. "Who is this?"

"Wayne Hewett. Charlene took a few days off to go to Florida," the man said. "Do you have an emergency?"

"Yes, sorry, um, there seems to be someone passed out in a snowbank. I tried to wake them, but got no response."

"Who is this?"

"I'm Allie McMurphy."

"Oh," he said. "*The* Allie McMurphy?"

"I guess, unless there's more than one of us."

"Where are you? I'll send first responders immediately."

"I'm at the ticket booth at the base of the stairs at Fort Mackinac," I said. "Listen, they're facedown in the snow. Should I try to turn them over?"

"Are they breathing?" he asked.

"I can't see their face," I said. "They're facedown in the snow." I felt strange repeating myself, but I had a feeling he wasn't understanding.

"Oh! See if you can gently turn them so that their face is uncovered."

"Are you sure I should turn them? What if they hurt their neck?"

"Ma'am, they may be drowning in snow. Try to clear the snow away from their face."

"Right," I said, and hit SPEAKER on my phone before I put it down on the top of the snow and carefully dug around the hooded figure. I could hear sirens in the distance. "I've dug out around their face, but I don't feel any breath."

"Allie, what's going on?"

I looked up to see Patrick Damon standing behind me. Patrick was the head of hospitality at the Grand Hotel. "Whoever this is, is facedown in the snow and unresponsive," I said, and pointed to my phone. "I called nine-one-one and help is on the way. But they may be suffocating."

"I'll help you turn them. Can you get around their head?"

I grabbed my phone and stuffed it in my pocket. Mal barked and dug at the snow. I managed to squeeze myself between the hooded head and the ticket booth wall. Patrick straddled the person's shoulders.

"Okay, on three I want you to hold their head steady and we'll turn them to the right. One, two, three."

We rolled the person over and the white face of a young woman appeared out of the snow. Her eyes were half-open and her face bloodless. Snow filled her mouth. "She's definitely not breathing." I used my fingers to scoop snow out of her mouth.

"I don't get a pulse," Patrick said as he felt the base of her neck. "Do you think she might be dead?"

"She could just be cold," I said. "We should try CPR."

"Allie, what's going on?" Mrs. Tunisian and Mrs. Schmidt came running up.

"It's Kayla Cramdon," Mrs. Schmidt said, and covered her mouth in shock.

"I'll call nine-one-one," Mrs. Tunisian said.

"I've already called," I said. "She's not breathing."

"I can do mouth-to-mouth," Mrs. Schmidt said, and hunkered down, pushing Patrick out of the way. She put her cheek by Kayla's mouth. "You're right, she isn't breathing." She felt for a pulse in her neck. "I can't get a heartbeat, but she's not stiff. I'm going to start CPR. Let's get her all the way on her back." She put one hand over the other, intertwined her fingers, and began steady, hard compressions.

The sirens in the distance got louder and louder as the ambulance approached. Automobiles were not allowed on Mackinac Island. It's part of what gave the island its "back in time" feel. The only exceptions were the ambulance, the fire truck and a plow. Safety first.

George Marron stepped out of the ambulance, grabbed his emergency kit, and pushed past the growing crowd. "What's going on?"

"I found her facedown in the snow. We turned her and Mrs. Schmidt started compressions," I said.

"How long was she without oxygen?"

"I don't know," I said. "Mal and I found her." My puppy, Mal, wagged her stub tail at the sound of her name.

"All right, let me in," George said. His copper skin shone in the sun and his long black hair was braided into a pigtail down his back. A second EMT I'd not met before hurried behind him with a backboard.

Rex Manning pulled up on a snowmobile at nearly the same time. He got off, removed his helmet, and addressed the crowd. "Everyone needs to step back. If you were not part of the original people on the scene, please go back to what you were doing." The crowd murmured but listened and started to thin.

Mal barked and wagged her tail, happy to see Rex. He had a grim look on his face and my heartbeat picked up. Rex looked every bit the action hero with his shaved head and well-muscled arms. The winter police uniform did little to hide his shape. He spotted me. His gaze moved from me to Mal and back, sending a frisson of excitement down my spine. The man had the most insane blue eyes ringed in thick black lashes.

"Allie, what happened?" He took out his notebook and studied George at work.

"Mal and I found her. I think Mrs. Schmidt said her name was Kayla. Anyway, we found her facedown in the snow. Patrick came by and helped me turn her over as carefully as possible. Then Mrs. Schmidt started CPR until George got here and took over."

"Do you know how she ended up in the snow-bank?"

"I don't," I said, and hugged my waist. "I didn't see anything until Mal found her."

"All right," he said, his tone even. "Stay here." He went over to Patrick next. Patrick was the same height as Rex, but much thinner. He must have been out jogging when he saw us because he was wearing cold-weather running gear. His spindly legs were covered in spandex and his coat didn't look heavy enough to do more than protect him from the wind.

Officer Charles Brown arrived next and after a brief exchange with Rex started to encourage the remaining crowd to break up and go back to their activities.

By the time the crowd had dispersed, Frances and Douglas came by.

"Allie, what's going on?"

"Mal and I found a woman facedown in the snow. I think it's Kayla Cramdon, well, that's what Mrs. Schmidt said. I met Kayla once or twice, but I barely remember her."

"Is she okay?" Frances asked as we watched the EMTs move her to a stretcher and roll her to the ambulance.

"I don't know. She wasn't breathing and I couldn't find a pulse so Mrs. Schmidt started CPR. They must have got her breathing again because they aren't bagging her."

"Poor thing," Frances said. "Any idea what happened?"

"None," I said, and watched the ambulance take off. "But it looks like she isn't dead and that's a huge relief." I turned to Frances and Douglas. "How's the light display coming?"

Frances was in her seventies but still going strong. She was dressed in snow boots, snow pants, and a parka. Her cheeks were rosy from the cold. Douglas was a year older than Frances and wore a plaid flannel shirt under his open Carhartt coat and bib overalls.

"We can still use your help," Douglas said.

"I'll be over there as soon as possible," I said.

They turned to go and I put my hand on Frances's arm. She stopped. "What?"

"Do you know of anyone who might not have known you moved out of your apartment?"

"No, it's pretty common knowledge that Douglas and I moved into the cottage. Why?"

"I got this message taped to the door this morning." I pulled out the paper and showed it to her. "It's why I'm here. I thought I could see what they wanted and then meet you all at the display."

She looked at the note but didn't touch it. "Who would write something so cryptic?"

"That's what I was hoping to find out. Did you know Kayla well?"

"No, we just met last week at a town hall meeting. We both liked the guest speaker—Albert Mann. Anyway, she said she'd only been on the island for a few months. I think she works at the Golden Goose Bar and Grill. Do you think she was the one who wrote the note?"

"I don't know," I said.

"What note?" Rex asked behind me.

I turned to see him studying me with an expressionless look. "This one," I said, and handed the note to him. He had gloves on and took it carefully. "Someone taped it to the door of Frances's apartment this morning. I didn't see who."

"Is this why you were here?"

"Yes," I said. "Do you think Kayla left it?"

"At this point there's no way to know for sure," he said.

I frowned. "Were they able to revive her? Is she going to be all right?" I looked at the ambulance as it rolled away from the scene.

"They're doing all that they can," he said. "Did you notice anything that might look like foul play?"

"No," I admitted. "I didn't see anyone near here. I was going to leave until Mal found her. I'm just glad she wasn't dead."

"But you think Kayla might be somehow connected to this note?"

"I don't know," I said, and I pulled thick mittens out of my coat pocket and put them on. My hands were frozen and my cheeks felt cold. "Most likely there's no connection. It's just a little odd, is all."

"What's odd?" he asked.

"Finding a note on my door and then no one being here when we arrive only to find Kayla in the snow. With my track record, it's hard to believe it isn't connected."

"You think someone wanted you to find Kayla?"

I looked at him. "Do you?"

"I'll keep the note in case it's connected." He pulled a plastic bag out of his pocket and slipped the note inside and sealed it. "I'll get it back to you if nothing's out of the ordinary."

"So can I go help with the display?"

"Yes."

I turned to leave and paused. "Rex?"

"Yes?"

"How's Melonie?" Melonie was Rex's second wife. She had turned up suddenly just before I was to move in with Rex. She needed his help and now it was Melonie and not me living in Rex's two-bedroom cottage.

"Doing better," he said, his expression unreadable.

"Good," I said and sent him a small smile. Then I turned and walked Mal through the trampled snow to the display area. Yes, Christmastime on Mackinac was sure proving to be different from what I imagined.

CHRISTMAS MUFFINS

1 cup unsalted butter
1 cup granulated sugar
2 eggs
1 teaspoon vanilla
1½ cups sifted flour
1½ teaspoons cinnamon
1 teaspoon ground cloves
1 cup walnuts, chopped fine
Powdered sugar

Heat oven to 350 degrees F. Generously grease and flour muffin tins. In a large bowl, cream butter and sugar until smooth. Add eggs one at a time and add vanilla. In a second bowl, mix flour, cinnamon, and cloves, then add to creamed mixture. Stir until well combined. Add nuts and stir again. Cover and chill 1 hour.

Scoop mixture into muffin tins. Bake 18 minutes or until light brown. Cool 10 minutes and remove from pan. When completely cool, dust with powdered sugar. For a lace look, place a doily on top and sift the sugar over. Carefully remove doily. Arrange on a plate and serve.

Makes 36 muffins.

Chapter 2

"It took a couple of hours, but the display looks pretty good, if you ask me," Frances said as she stepped back and eyed our completed creation. Mal barked in agreement. The display was cheerfully lit and the sun had gone down, leaving only the cold, the snow, and the twinkling lights. Our outline of Main Street was evident and Douglas had made the lights on the wheels of the horse-drawn carriage look as if they were revolving by blinking in a circular sequence.

"I like it," I admitted, standing with my arms crossed. It was crazy how warm it had felt when we were working and had the sun on our backs, but now that the sun had set, I realized that my cheeks were numb and my words came out a bit slurred.

"Why don't you and Mal come back to our place for a nice cup of hot cocoa?" Douglas suggested. "You've earned it."

"Sure," I said. "I'll stop at Doud's and pick up something for dessert." Doud's was the oldest grocer on Mackinac Island and wasn't too far away from the light competition.

"Just not ice cream," Frances said. "I think four hours outside in the cold is enough."

"Fine," I said. "Come on, Mal." I left the newlyweds to make their way back to their new house and took a quick trip to Doud's. Mal and I entered the crowded store. I loved the old-time feel of Doud's. They had wooden shelves and high ceilings covered in tin squares. Doud's offered hot food from the kitchen in the back with a modern salad bar.

It seemed that there were quite a few people with the same idea, as the store was filled with community members grabbing something hot to stave off the cold. I snatched up the last coconut cake from the bakery and Mal and I made our way to the checkout.

"Hey, Allie, I heard you found another body today."

I glanced over my shoulder to see Betty Olway. Betty was a tall woman with a thin face. She wore a snowsuit and a knitted cap that let a few of her long gray curls spill out.

"Oh no, it was Kayla Cramdon and she wasn't dead," I said.

"That's not the story we heard," Mary Emry said. Mary worked as the main cashier at Doud's. She was a little shorter than me with dark hair and brown eyes. She didn't usually say much so I was surprised by her interjection into the conversation.

"They took her off in the ambulance," I said.

"Last I heard she was warming up and breathing on her own."

"Well, will wonders never cease," Betty said. "This is the first time I've ever heard of you finding someone who was still alive." She glanced down at Mal. "Are dogs allowed in Doud's?"

"We're just getting dessert," I said, and handed my money to Mary, who had rung up my cake. "I wasn't going to leave her in the street."

"You should get one of those dog carriers that go on your back," Betty commented. "Dogs should not be allowed in stores."

"We're leaving." I picked up my cake and left the grocer. The streets were cold and quiet. I could hear the sound of music coming from one of the bars. Lights from inside the few open businesses brightened the snow-covered street. There were snowmobiles parked outside the bar but no carriages waited for riders.

Mal and I hurried the few blocks up the hill and beyond the fort to Frances's new place. Her street was homier than Main Street. The houses were smaller than the showy grand cottages along the lakefront. Instead they were tiny bungalows nestled side by side. People had them decorated with multicolored lights. It smelled of new snow. That particular scent of winter brought back a rush of holiday memories.

Mal wasted no time in dragging me to the right home and up the small porch. I knocked at the door just under the fresh pine wreath.

"Come on in," Douglas said as he opened the door.

The warmth of the inside hit my cheeks and made me smile. I handed him the cake box. "I hope you like coconut." Then I pulled off my hat and gloves and kicked off my boots, leaving them in the boot tray by the door. Mal waited patiently for me to hang up my coat on the nearby coat tree. Then I took off her pink coat, harness, and leash, and wiped her feet to free them of snow balls. The last thing I wanted was for her to track snow through Frances's new home.

"Come in," Frances said as she entered the room with a tray full of drinks in her hands. "Stop fussing, you can't hurt anything."

I straightened and Mal took off to beg Douglas for attention. There was a fire in the cozy fireplace. Just past the small tiled entry area was a warmly decorated living room. Frances had hung sheer curtains and then wide panels of dark green velvet that swooped to each side held back by cords. A couch and a love seat faced each other beside the fireplace. They were overstuffed with large-pink-cabbage-rose-patterned material that had a pale green background. The walls were painted a matching pale green. Frances had Christmas decorations up with old-timey Santas, and a manger scene with angels. She placed the tray on the coffee table between the two seats.

"I've got the cake," Douglas said as he came out

with the cake on a cake stand, a cake knife and server in hand.

Mal followed him into the room and jumped up on the couch beside Frances.

"Get down, silly," I ordered as I took a seat on the love seat across from Frances. Mal jumped down as I had asked, only to jump up beside me.

Frances picked up a cup and poured in coffee then handed it to me. "I wonder how Kayla is doing."

I took the cup and added cream while Douglas cut the cake. "I saw Betty Olway at Doud's. She seemed to think Kayla died." I pulled out my phone and checked my texts. "I haven't heard from Rex, though."

"Seems like he would let you know before anyone could tell Betty," Douglas said, and passed me a slice of cake. Mal's nose twitched so I reached into my pocket and pulled out a dog treat. I motioned for her to get down. After she did, I gave her the treat and she took it and sat down to snack, allowing me to eat my cake in peace.

"I wouldn't worry about it until we hear from Rex," Frances said. "It's close to Christmas and I, for one, believe in the miracle of the season." She handed Douglas a coffee and he traded her for a plate with a slice of cake.

"You said that you just met Kayla. I didn't recognize her at first. Then I remembered where I knew her from. She was part of the group of volunteers who helped remove the debris from the McMurphy. After it was all removed, I went to each volunteer's home to hand-deliver thank-you fudge. Kayla lived in an apartment behind Main Street. I remember that the furniture looked old but she was young and new to the island, so I think her apartment might have been furnished when she rented it."

"If she lives in the Ambassador apartments, they are fully furnished," Douglas said. "Most of the apartments are furnished, you know. It's really expensive to ship things over to the island."

"Huh," I took a bite of cake and savored the flavor of coconut. The cake had a chocolate fudge filling. "I hadn't thought about it. I mean, my apartment was furnished with Grammy and Papa's things when I first got here. I know it was crazy getting new mattresses this fall. But I've been buying boxed furniture for when I move back into the McMurphy. Shipping hasn't been terribly expensive, although it might take some time for me to build everything once I'm allowed back into the McMurphy."

"You should hire someone to help you. Insurance should help cover any expense," Frances said. "On the bright side it will be fun for you to decorate the place to your liking."

"I do have to admit; I've been online studying some small-space apartment designs."

"You're lucky it's so easy to design and furnish with the Internet. We used to have to read magazines and cut out pictures to put things together."

"Well, you did a lovely job with this place." I made a point to look around.

"It's a mash-up of some of my stuff and Douglas's

things," Frances said. "With only a few things like curtains and rugs to pull it all together."

"Well, it looks cozy and harmonious."

"It's because we like the same things," Douglas said between bites of cake.

We sat in comfortable silence for a moment and my thoughts went back to Kayla. "Frances, do you think that Kayla was the one to leave a note on your door and ask you to meet her in the park?"

Frances put down her fork. "You know, I was thinking about that. I really didn't know her. Besides, young people these days would just text."

I put my empty cake plate on the coffee table. "Did she have your cell number?"

"No," Frances said. "Like I said, we only met the one time."

"Maybe she did leave the note, then," I mused. Mal jumped up in my lap and I petted her absently. There was something about her warm little body that comforted me.

"Maybe the note was meant for you," Douglas said. "I'm sure Kayla didn't have your number, either."

"True. If so, what do you think she wanted from me?" I asked. "Why not just wait for me to answer the door and chat face-to-face?"

"It does seem odd," Frances answered. She sent Douglas a look. "You said they knocked? Why not just talk to you, then? Why meet you at the steps to the fort?"

"I thought maybe they wanted to talk to me about

the lighting display, you know, show me something there . . ."

"Then maybe it wasn't Kayla at all," Frances said, and frowned.

"If it wasn't Kayla, then who was it?"

"I'd say speculating about any of this will just run you down a rabbit hole," Douglas said, and put down his cake plate. "Is there a way to know for sure it was Kayla who left you the note?"

"She didn't sign it, if that's what you're asking," I said, and chewed on the inside of my lip. "I suppose it could have been anyone, really. It's strange, though, that no one showed up and then we found Kayla facedown in the snowbank like that."

"Could be a coincidence," Frances said, and sipped coffee.

"Maybe," I agreed.

"Well, you can't let speculation keep you up at night," Douglas said.

"But we're speculating we are going to win the lighting contest," Frances said with a twinkle in her eyes.

"Good speculation can happen anytime," Douglas said. He put his arms around Frances.

"Okay," I said, and stood. Mal jumped down and circled my feet. "You're right. We really don't know if there is a connection between the note and Kayla's accident. Listen, I should get going."

"You should take home some of the leftover cake," Frances said as she stood.

"Oh no, there are two of you and only one of me. I don't think I need that much cake."

Frances walked me to the door and rubbed my arm. "It's going to be okay."

"I certainly hope you're right." I gave her a quick hug and put on my snow gear and Mal's coat and leash. "Thanks for having me over."

"You're always welcome, dear," Frances said.

Mal and I stepped out into the clear cold night only to run straight into Rex.

"Watch yourself," he said as he steadied me.

"Rex, what brings you here?" Frances asked as Rex reluctantly let go of me.

"We need to talk," Rex said to Frances. "May I come in?"

"Of course." Frances opened the door wider to invite him in.

"Is everything all right?" I asked.

"Go home, Allie," Rex advised as he stepped inside and took off his hat.

"Frances?"

"I'm sure it's fine," Frances said. "Go home and get some rest. You have fudge to make in the morning."

"Are you sure? I can be here for you if you need me," I said, and craned my neck to see Rex slipping off his boots and Douglas coming over to chat with him.

Frances sent me a gentle smile. "I'm sure. Go home."

She shut the door behind me and I blew out a cloudy breath. "Come on, Mal," I said. "We know when we're being dismissed." We walked through the crunchy snow to Main Street.

There was a chill wind off the lake that made me

put the hood of my parka up. The street was quiet except for the lights from the bar on the corner. Tomorrow was Wednesday and they would put a tree up in the middle of Main Street and encourage the community to come out and decorate it. Then there would be the official lighting of the displays and tree. Followed by judging, awards, and plenty of hot cocoa and mulled wine.

I walked by the McMurphy. I barely recognized it without the lights on. The fourth floor had been reframed and the roof built with heavy-duty joists for the rooftop deck I had permitted. A small sadness filled my heart. If I had not tried to reinforce the roof, then the McMurphy might still be livable. Now it looked lonely. The front siding was mismatched until spring, when it would be warm enough to paint.

"It's Christmas," I muttered into the quiet air. "Stop being so maudlin. After all, the McMurphy will be shiny and new for the next season and filled with possibility."

"Hey, Allie," Officer Brown said as he walked by then stopped. He caught me studying the McMurphy. "It's so great that the community came together to help you get the roof on before the first big snow."

I smiled at the memory. "Yes, it was. So many people turned out. It was like an old-fashioned barn raising."

"People like you. They want to help."

"Thanks for the reminder," I said. My spirits lifted. "I needed it."

"Anytime," he said, and tipped his hat then turned to go.

"Say," I said, stopping him. He turned back to me with a question in his gaze. "How is Kayla?"

His face went solemn. "I'm afraid she didn't make it."

"Oh no, that's terrible. What about her family?"

"Sophie flew her mother in an hour ago. She was there when Kayla passed."

"I'm so sorry to hear that," I said. "Do you know what happened?"

"That information hasn't been released yet," Officer Brown said. "There will be a statement made in the morning."

"Is that why Rex went to see Frances? Frances told me she didn't really know Kayla. They'd only just met at the last town hall meeting."

"I can't say," Officer Brown said. "Rex will be releasing a statement later." His gaze went to Mal. "I think your pup is cold. You should probably get home. I heard there's a storm coming."

"Right." I picked Mal up and tucked her under my arm. "Thanks." Then I hurried home. Mal was indeed shivering even though she wore her little pink coat. There wasn't anything I could do hanging out on the cold street. When I got home, I planned to text Douglas and see if he might tell me why Rex came to see them.

I stepped into the center hallway of my new home and put Mal down. She shook off the snow as best she could while I unlocked the apartment door. I slipped off my boots and set them in the boot tray just inside the door. Mal ran inside and I stopped her by grabbing the end of her leash. "Oh no, you don't," I said, and gently reeled her toward me. "We have to get the snow balls off your legs."

I flipped the switch and the overhead light in the large open living area came to life, causing Mella to stretch and jump down from her perch at the top of the cat tree. I closed the door behind me and took time to study the ice balls in Mal's curly fur. My pup loved the snow, but it tended to tangle in her fur and create ice. I had two choices: carefully untangle it myself or throw her in the bathtub and let warm water wash it out.

After the hours we'd been outside, I decided to go the bath route. I quickly hung up my coat and said hello to Mella, who meowed her displeasure at being left alone so long.

"I know, I missed dinner," I said. "Let's take care of one thing at a time." Picking up Mal, I headed to the bathroom off the kitchen. The apartment was quiet and warmed by radiators. I pulled back the shower curtain, put Mal in the bath, and turned on the water. She wasn't happy and tried to scramble out. Before long, I was soaked, but Mal was free of ice and towel-dried. She raced off into the apartment like a kid fresh from a bath.

I caught a glance of myself in the mirror. My wavy hair was stuck to my head on top and frizzy on the bottom. I had mascara rings under my eyes and my cheeks were definitely windburned. Sighing, I climbed out of my wet jeans and T-shirt, wrapped myself in my thick old robe, and headed through the kitchen to the bedroom. I wish the builders, when they remodeled the old Victorian into apartments, had thought to put a door between the bathroom and the bedroom. As it stood now, the bathroom was beside the bedroom closet, but you had to walk around, through the kitchen, through the living area, to get into the bedroom, which was behind the kitchen. I was lucky to have a brick fireplace in the far corner of the living area. I had loaded it up with fresh wood earlier and considered having a fire and making popcorn. I really wanted to just get cozy on the couch with my pets.

There was a knock at my door as I dug leggings out of my dresser. "I'll be right there," I shouted as Mal barked. I slid an oversize sweatshirt on. There was a second knock and Mal was turning circles barking and jumping at the door. I hurried into the leggings. "Just a second." I raced to the door.

A quick peek out the viewer told me it was Maggs at the front door. Margaret Vanderbilt was Frances's best friend. I opened the door. "Maggs, what's wrong?"

She looked stricken and out of breath. "It's Frances. Have you not checked your phone?"

"No," I said, and turned to figure out where I left my phone. "Watch, don't let the cat out," I called. The door shut and Maggs stood against it. Mella was a bit miffed as she rubbed up against Maggs. I grabbed my phone and saw I had missed five texts. I turned to Maggs. "What's happened?"

"Rex has taken Frances into custody."

"What? Why?" My heartbeat picked up.

"It has to do with Kayla's death. They don't think it was an accident." Maggs fanned her flushed cheeks. The woman was wearing a parka and corduroy pants.

"Why Frances?" I shoved my bare feet into my boots and gathered up my parka. I fully intended to go down to the police station and give Rex a piece of my mind.

"Douglas wasn't sure," Maggs said. "So I made some phone calls on the way over here. It seems that Kayla was conscious enough to say one thing before she passed."

"What?"

"She said Frances's name."

Chapter 3

Maggs and I trudged through the cold dark streets toward the police station, our breath puffs of vapor in the air. I'd stopped long enough to feed my pets before I raced out the door. But I hadn't taken the time to put on socks or gather my gloves and I regretted it.

"Did you talk to Frances?" I asked, my lips numb.

"Douglas called me," she said. "Right after he called a lawyer."

"Did he say if Frances was okay?"

"He said she was taking it like Frances," Maggs said.

I glanced at her. Her face held a tight expression. It seemed ever since her son was killed Maggs's expression rarely softened. I wondered if this new turn of events brought it all back. "Everything is going to be all right," I said.

"From your mouth to God's ears," Maggs replied. We arrived at the white administration building/police station and went inside. Douglas paced in the small area in front of the front desk.

"Douglas, what happened?" I asked as I stomped snow off my boots and hurried to him.

"Rex wouldn't tell me anything other than that he needed to take Frances down here for questioning." Douglas looked grim. "I asked him what it was about and he said, Kayla's death."

"Why aren't you with her?" Maggs asked.

"They wouldn't let me back there," Douglas said.

"Is the lawyer here yet?" I asked.

"I called her cousin the lawyer, but he lives in the Lower Peninsula," Douglas said. "He can't be here until tomorrow morning."

"Surely there's a lawyer on the island," I replied. "I don't want Frances here all night."

"I agree," Douglas said.

"Michael O'Dea is a retired lawyer," Maggs said. "He's here visiting his daughter for the holidays. I'll call him." She pulled out her cell phone and went over to the windows to make the call.

I clung to Douglas's arm. He had taken off his parka and hung it on the back of one of the plastic waiting room chairs. "It's going to be okay," I said to stem both of our worry. "Rex is pretty impartial. He may be bringing in other people to question. In fact, he may want to see me next."

"I hate feeling helpless," Douglas grumbled.

"Me, too," I said. "Excuse me." I unzipped my coat and went over to the officer on desk duty. "Hello." I glanced at the man's name tag. "Officer Hatch, is it?"

"What can I do for you?" he asked. Officer Hatch

looked like he was maybe twenty-one years old and fresh out of the police academy.

"Can you tell me why Officer Manning is questioning Frances Devaney?"

"It has to do with the Kayla Cramdon murder investigation," he said. "That's all I can tell you."

"What does Frances have to do with Kayla's death?"

"Like I said"—he looked down at the desktop monitor—"there isn't anything else I can tell you."

"Well, it was worth a try," I said, and blew out a breath. "Is Officer Lasko on duty?"

"She gets in at eight a.m."

"What about Officer Brown?"

"He's on foot patrol," Officer Hatch said without taking his eyes from his screen. He started typing and seemed impervious to my concern.

"Michael is on his way," Maggs said.

"Good," Douglas replied as I rejoined them. He turned to me. "You found Kayla. Is there anything you can think of that would tie her death to Frances?"

"No," I said. "You were with Frances all morning, right?"

His face went still.

"No?" I asked as my heartbeat picked up.

"I left to work on the Christmas lighting an hour early. I had to get the cutouts installed so that you two could hang the lights."

"When was that?" I asked, and took off my parka.

"We had breakfast at eight and I left at ten. Frances arrived at the display site at noon." He looked at me.

"We noticed the ambulance about ten minutes later and came to check on you."

"So there are two hours when you didn't see Frances," I said.

"Yes."

"I saw her," Maggs said. "Well, we talked on the phone."

"When?" I asked, trying to figure out what Rex suspected.

"About ten-thirty," Maggs said. "We chatted about stuff and nonsense."

"How did she seem?" I asked.

"Fine." Maggs shook her head. "She was busy doing laundry and such."

"When did you hang up?"

"About eleven-thirty a.m.," Maggs said. "Frances had to go because someone was at the door."

"Do you know who that was?" I asked.

"No," Maggs said. "Sadly, I don't."

"So Frances doesn't have an alibi," I muttered.

"She shouldn't need one," Douglas groused. "Everyone knows Frances wouldn't hurt a flea."

The door opened and a rather tall, thin, older man walked in. He wore an overcoat and thick boots with jeans. His head was covered in an orange hunter's cap with earflaps pulled down.

"Oh, thank goodness, you're here, Michael," Maggs said, and hugged him. He awkwardly patted her back.

"You do realize I studied corporate law, not criminal law," Michael said in a low rumbly voice.

"I trust you will do well," Maggs said, and turned toward Douglas. "Douglas Devaney, meet Michael O'Dea."

The two men shook hands and sized each other up.

"And this is Allie McMurphy," Maggs said.

"Nice to meet you," he said, and shook my hand. He'd pulled off his gloves and his hands were large and warm.

"Now, where's my client?" he asked.

"They won't tell us where they took her," Douglas said grimly.

"Don't worry," Michael said, and patted Douglas on the shoulder. "I'll find out what's going on and get her safely home." Michael walked over to the desk officer and with minimal words, had the man up on his feet. He opened the door to the back and disappeared down the hall.

"There's nothing for us to do now but wait," I said as I pulled Maggs down to sit with me in the green plastic chairs. "Take your coat off before you overheat and try not to worry."

"That's going to be difficult." She pulled off her parka and held it in her lap.

"It's Frances," I reassured her. "She'll come through this with shining colors."

It took two hours before Michael emerged with Frances on his arm. Douglas grabbed her and looked her in the eyes. "Are you all right?"

"I'm fine," Frances said, but she sounded tired.

"What happened?" I asked. "What did Rex want?"

"They wanted to question her about what happened today," Michael said. "They were clearly fishing."

"It's late," Frances said. "I'm exhausted. Can we just go home?"

"Certainly," Douglas said.

"Would you like us to go home with you?" I asked. "I can make a nice tea . . ."

"Thank you both for being here for me," Frances said. "But it really is late and I have Douglas. Why don't you both go home and get some sleep? I'll answer all your questions in the morning."

"Are you sure?" I asked, and worried my bottom lip between my teeth.

"I'm certain," she said. "Come on, Douglas."

"I'll walk you both home," Michael said.

"Allie, you'll see to Maggs, right?" Frances asked. She looked pale. Her big brown eyes were shadowed with something I couldn't quite make out.

"Of course," I said. "We'll call you in the morning." We put on our coats and outdoor gear.

"Good night," Frances said as we stepped out into the cold. Frances, Douglas, and Michael walked one way and Maggs and I turned the other. When we were sufficiently far enough away I glanced at Maggs. "So what do you think we should do?"

"Frances will tell me what happened," Maggs said. "Don't fret. Once she does, we'll formulate a plan on how to help. For now, let's go home and go to bed. You have fudge to make in the morning."

I gave her a slight smile. "You mean in a few hours. How about I walk you home."

"Oh no, you shouldn't be walking yourself home alone. There's a killer on the loose."

"It's Mackinac Island," I said with a shrug. "It's safe."

"Tell Kayla that."

Sugar Cookie Fudge

18–24 sugar cookies, unfrosted (I like homemade, but store-bought is fine—even better if you bake some premixed.)
1 16-ounce can vanilla frosting
1 package small colorful sprinkles (I like the tiny, colored candy balls.)
1 12-ounce package vanilla baking chips

Line an 8 x 8-inch pan with parchment paper or foil. Butter pan.

In a food processor, pulse cookies into crumbs. Add ⅓ cup frosting and 2 tablespoons sprinkles. Mix well, measure ½-teaspoon drops, and roll into balls.

In a medium microwaveable bowl, microwave vanilla chips on high for 1 minute. Add remaining frosting. Microwave 30 seconds and stir. If necessary, microwave 15 more seconds and stir until smooth.

Pour half of fudge mixture into pan. Push the cookie balls into the fudge mixture then pour remaining half of fudge mixture over the top. Add sprinkles. Pat into mixture. Chill until set. Cut into 1-inch squares and serve. Store in an airtight container.

Makes 64 squares.

Chapter 4

Up just a few hours later, I worked all morning making fudge. It was hard to not reach for my phone and bug Frances. I packed up my boxes for shipping, harnessed Mal, and we left the apartment to put the fudge orders in the mail. Outside the sun shone brightly and the snow reflected a pure blue sky.

Later tonight would be the Christmas tree decorating party and then the lighting ceremony. I'd promised Douglas I'd come and help him put the finishing touches on our light display.

"Allie," Rex called my name.

"Rex," I said. I didn't know how mad I should be at him for questioning Frances and worse, not telling me he was going to take her to the station last night.

"About yesterday . . ."

"If you knew you were going to take Frances to the station, you should have let me stay and go with her for support." That statement came out a touch more accusing than I wanted.

"I wanted to talk to you about the note and about Kayla."

"Are you going to take me to the station to be grilled as well?"

"Allie."

I sighed. "I've got to ship my fudge."

"I'll walk with you."

I let silence grow thick between us as we headed to the shipping store. The boxes would be air-flighted out and then given to a distribution hub where they would go overnight to their destination. I ensured I made flavors that would survive two days in case the overnight shipment got stuck somewhere.

"How's Melonie doing?" I asked, unable to stop myself from breaking the silence. I shouldn't have. He deserved to understand how miffed I was with him.

"She's working through some things," he said gruffly.

"Huh," was all I said. We walked another two blocks in silence and, when I spotted the shipping office, I sped up. He kept pace and opened the door for me. Mal trotted in beside us as I put the packages down on the counter.

"Hi, Sandy," I said. Sandy Sechrest was a retired librarian who now owned and ran the small shipping shop on Market Street. She had white hair with turquoise streaks in her bangs. Rumor was that she had gone white at an early age. The turquoise color was stunning against her lovely white hair.

"Hello, Allie," she said. "Just these five boxes today?"

"That's it," I said. "It's getting close to Christmas.

I think sales are dropping off a bit as everyone is worried it won't arrive in time."

She looked at me. "Did you mention an order cutoff day for guaranteed arrival by Christmas on your website? We have guaranteed shipping through the twenty-third."

"Oh, that's a good idea," I said. "I wish I had thought of that. I'll do it. Thanks for the tip."

"Hi, Rex," she said as she weighed the boxes and slapped labels on them. "I heard Kayla Cramdon passed last night. Such a shame. She was so young."

Rex cleared his throat. "Yes, well, sounds like the rumor mill is working just fine today."

"You should have announced it at a press meeting," I said, and gave him a side eye.

"We did," he said. "A press release went out early this morning."

"I bet Liz McElroy was happy to get the story in time for the afternoon paper. That was so thoughtful of you," I said to Rex, and paid my bill.

"Here's your receipt, Allie. We heard that Kayla was possibly a victim of foul play," Sandy said. "Allie, are you going to investigate?"

"She is not," Rex said when I opened my mouth to speak.

I closed my mouth and took my receipt. "I'll see you tomorrow, Sandy."

"Bye, Allie. Bye, Rex."

Mal barked.

"Oh yes," Sandy said. "Good-bye, Mal. I'll see you tomorrow."

We walked outside into the cold bright sunlight.

Mal danced around the edges of the snowbank, sniffing to see who had passed by while we were inside.

"Come to the station with me," Rex said.

I shielded my eyes from the blinding sun with my free hand. "Am I going to need a lawyer?" I asked. "I think Michael O'Dea is the resident lawyer at the moment."

"You aren't going to need a lawyer," Rex said softly. "You aren't a suspect."

"Then why do I have to go in for questioning?"

"We can do it out here if you want to freeze while getting a sunburn."

"Fine," I said, and headed toward the police station. "But Mal is not going to jail."

"Neither are you," he said softly.

We approached the admin building and Rex reached around to open the door for us. "Can I get you a coffee?"

I stomped the snow off my boots and took off my hat and gloves. Mal shook her body, releasing a small mountain of snow. Rex shepherded us through the door to the back and into a small conference room.

"Make yourself comfortable," he said. "I'll get you a coffee and Mal some water."

He stepped out, closing the door behind him. Sighing, I took off my coat and hung it on the back of a chair. I sat down and Mal jumped into my lap. So I gave her a nice scratch behind her ears. The conference room was small and had a single table with a Formica top and four metal chairs around it.

The room was painted a faded beige and in need of a fresh coat. The ceiling was an old drop ceiling with a fluorescent light that buzzed. It was not a comfortable room and I was pretty sure it wasn't meant to be comfortable.

The door opened and Rex stepped into the room, closing the door behind him. He'd removed his coat and gloves and his hands were full. He set a paper cup with coffee down in front of me. "Cream, no sugar," he said with a small smile. "I have water and a dog treat for Mal." He put a small bowl of water on the floor and Mal jumped down. She did a neat pirouette for the treat.

"Can you tell me why you dragged Frances into the station last night?" I asked, and wrapped my hands around the cup to warm them.

"You know I can't," he said. "Kayla Cramdon died yesterday and we are pretty sure it wasn't natural causes."

"But you don't know because they haven't done an autopsy," I surmised, and sipped the hot coffee. It was particularly strong and bitter even with the creamer.

"It's an ongoing investigation," he said. "I should point out that this is being videotaped."

"Why am I here?"

"I want to go over again how you found Kayla."

"I told you."

"There might be something else you remember. Something different. I'd like to go over everything from the beginning for the record."

I blew out a long breath and told him again about how I had plans to help Frances and Douglas with our entry. That I was making fudge when the doorbell rang, but no one was there. Only a note taped to the door.

"Is there a security camera in the foyer of the building?" he asked, and took notes on a scratch pad. I tried to see what he was writing, but it appeared to be shorthand.

"No," I said. "There really is no need for one."

"Until now," he said gently. "I suppose Frances doesn't have a security system in the apartment."

"No."

"What happened after you read the note?"

I repeated how I finished my fudge and Mal and I went to the meeting place mentioned in the note.

"You were going to meet someone but you didn't know who and you didn't tell anyone that you were doing this?" He made it sound as if I had been naive and unsafe.

"They asked to meet me in a public place, outside and within the eyes and ears of everyone who was working on their Christmas lighting displays. It was perfectly reasonable to go and see who it was. I really thought they were looking for Frances and I was going to take them to her."

"For all the investigations you've been involved in, you never think to take precautions?"

I narrowed my eyes and tilted my head. "Is that a rhetorical question?"

He frowned and blew out a breath. "You need to stop going places without people knowing."

"I don't know if you've noticed, but I'm not a child."

"I know you're not a child." His gaze grew hot for a moment and I could feel thick tension in the room. Then he looked down at his notes and when he looked back up his eyes were flat and cop-like. "So you took Mal to the spot at the bottom of the stairs that lead to the fort."

At the sound of her name, Mal jumped back up into my lap and I scratched her behind the ears. "Yes, and I didn't see anyone. In fact, I think I stood there for a whole five minutes. It's a nice spot for seeing people approaching and no one was waiting for me there."

"Except Kayla," he said.

"Well, I didn't know she was there." I felt a twinge in my heart. "Maybe if I'd seen her right away she would still be here."

"I'm pretty sure there was nothing you could have done."

"Why?" I asked.

"I can't give the particulars until after the autopsy," he said. "How did you find Kayla?"

"Mal pulled me around the corner of the ticket shack and I found her. I called for help and people came running. You know the rest."

"Did you see anyone around the ticket shack while you were walking up?"

"No."

"Did you notice anyone walking away from the steps?" he asked.

"Sadly, no," I said. "I don't remember even seeing tracks in the snow, well, besides Kayla's and my own."

"Fine, I guess that's it, then." He closed his notebook. "I strongly suggest you get security for the apartment while you're there."

"Oh, I really don't think that's necessary," I said. "I hope to move back into the McMurphy next week."

"The repairs must be coming along quickly."

After a fast smile I said, "The roof is on and the outside is buttoned up for winter. They restored my apartment's ceiling and are bringing in new cabinets and counters for the kitchen this week. Drywall goes up today and the appliances are scheduled to come in. Plus, the bathroom should be up and running." I sighed. "It's a shame they couldn't save the original claw-foot tub and pedestal sink. Unfortunately, they were shattered by the impact of the roof collapse."

"They've gotten a lot of work done quickly," he noted.

"It's been forty days," I pointed out. "But yes, everyone has been so helpful pitching in. I've been spending my afternoons painting and Douglas taught me a lot about pipes and plumbing and electricity. The permits and inspections are what take the longest."

"Will you wait until spring to reopen the hotel?"

"No, I'm pushing for occupancy in time to have guests for the Santa Fun Run in less than two weeks."

"That's ambitious," he said.

I stood. "You know I don't like to do things halfway. Do you need anything else?"

He got to his feet and opened the door. "You're free to go. Thank you for your cooperation."

I put Mal down on the floor and tugged on my coat. As I stepped into the hallway, Rex stopped me.

"Watch after Frances," he said, his voice low. "She's going to need friends."

"What does that mean?" I asked.

"I'm sure you know your way out," he replied. "Thanks again."

"Right," I said. Mal and I made our way down the short hall and out into the front waiting area. Outside the sky was dazzling blue and the air that crisp wet of new snow and lakeshore. I dialed Frances's number but it went straight to voice mail.

Frowning, I decided to walk over to the newspaper office and see if Liz could give me more details on Kayla Cramdon's death.

The newspaper building was small and neat. Someone had used a snowblower to clear the short path to the main door. There was thick rock salt spread over the sidewalk and between that and the sun, the pavement was quite dry.

I opened the door and wiped my feet on the heavy boot rug just inside the door. Mal didn't have to shake anything off this time as most of the sidewalks were wet and snow no longer clung to her fur.

"Hello?" I called.

Liz came out from the back. "Allie! So glad to see you." She walked around the tall front counter and gave me a hug. Then she bent down to give Mal a scratch under her chin. "What a year we're having on the island."

"That's what I came to talk to you about," I said. "Did you know that Rex pulled Frances into the police station last night for questioning?"

"I did," she said. "Come on back to the break room. I've got warm beverages and some coffee cake. We can talk in private."

"Sounds good to me." Mal and I followed her back. The back of the newspaper building still held a production area with an old-fashioned black-and-white printing press. I knew it wasn't used anymore as everything had gone digital. They printed using digital files and copiers now. Jared Fox ran the production equipment and was currently in the back working on the latest copy.

We wandered to the far back, where a tiny kitchen and break area was set up. I unzipped my coat and pulled it off, draping it over the plastic orange chair that must have been nearly fifty years old.

"Coffee or tea?" she asked me.

"Coffee, please," I said, and sat down. "I just came out of the police station myself."

"Why?" she asked as she poured coffee into two thick white mugs and set them on the table—one in front of me and one in front of the chair she took. Mal jumped up on my lap and happily eyed the cake stand where a half of a lovely coffee cake sat under a glass dome.

"Rex wanted me to go over how I found Kayla again. I don't know why," I said, and poured a generous helping of cream in my coffee. "Nothing in it changed."

Liz pulled two small plates from a stack beside the

cake and lifted the glass dome. Then she cut thick slices and placed them carefully, one on each plate. Covering the cake, she pushed the plate toward me, handed me a fork, and then dug into her cake.

I followed her example. It was a rich blueberry cinnamon coffee cake with walnuts and brown sugar crumble. "This is so good."

"Mrs. Tunisian brought it. I think she was trying to bribe me for details into Kayla's death."

"Did it work?" I asked.

Liz laughed. "No. If I told her anything, then she would tell everyone and I wouldn't have a paper to sell."

"She gave you the cake anyway?"

"Are you kidding me? There was no way I was giving this back," she said, and forked up another rich bite.

Mal settled onto the floor beside my chair and I put down my fork and took a sip of coffee. "What can you tell me about Kayla's death? I'm pretty certain it was suspicious, but Rex will only tell me that it was an ongoing investigation."

"I heard from Jenny at the clinic that they suspect Kayla was poisoned," Liz said. "They think that due to the poison, she had a dizzy spell and then fell into the snow and blacked out."

"That's terrible," I said, and sat back. "So it was murder."

"Most likely," Liz said. "They haven't ruled out accidental death yet. She had been taking some medicine for pain and anxiety."

"So, why Frances?" I asked.

"I'm not sure," Liz said. "Jenny couldn't tell me too many details. But I did hear from Ralph that Kayla did regain consciousness for a brief time before she passed. Rumor is that she only said one thing."

I leaned in closer. "I heard something about that. What did you hear?"

"She said Frances Wentworth's name."

Chapter 5

"That's what I heard," I said. "Do you know why? I didn't even know she knew Frances."

"I don't know why she said that, but I bet that's why Rex brought Frances in last night," Liz said, and picked up her coffee to take a sip.

"You think he thinks Frances had something to do with Kayla's death?"

"That was my guess," Liz said. "What did Frances say?"

"Nothing," I said. "She refused to talk to me. I'm meeting Maggs in a little bit. I'm hoping she told Maggs something about what Rex wanted and maybe how Frances is connected to Kayla."

"I haven't been able to find a connection," Liz said. "I have access to public records, but I wasn't able to find any records that link Kayla and Frances."

"I assume Kayla was born and raised on Mackinac Island?"

"No, actually, she wasn't," Liz said. "I did a little digging. It seems that Kayla was born in Saginaw, Michigan. Her parents divorced when she was ten.

Kayla rented her apartment on the island about two months ago and got a job at the Golden Goose at the end of the season, which is weird. Most people leave the island after the season is over. Kayla moved here then."

"Are her parents still alive? Do you know if they know Frances?"

"I understand that Kayla's mother came in on a charter plane with Sophie," Liz said. "She's staying at the Island Hotel for a week. Kayla's father is on a business trip and will come as soon as he can.

"Besides working at the bar, Kayla freelanced as a graphic artist, right?" I asked.

"Yes, how did you know that?"

"Kayla was one of the people who came to help haul away debris so we could raise the roof at the McMurphy. I took her thank-you fudge, but I haven't really had a reason to get to know her beyond that."

"Yes, she was a freelancer. She did some ads for the paper. I got to know her a little bit," Liz said. Liz had a head of gorgeous brown curls. She liked to wear flannel shirts and jeans with boots, but couldn't give up being girly. It showed in the intricate patterns on her manicured nails. This month she had tiny Christmas trees with packages under them. "Kayla told me that she learned that she might have family on Mackinac, but her mother wouldn't tell her about it. It seems her mother hates the island. When she asked her mother about the possibility of family here, her mother refused to talk about it."

"Has she ever been to Mackinac?"

"I couldn't find any record of it," Liz said. "I even looked up her mom's maiden name—Homestead. But there is no record of any Homesteads ever living here."

"It seems strange to me that anyone would dislike Mackinac Island—especially if they've never been here," I said, and thought about Rex. "I mean, some people can't tolerate the winters, but the easy fix for that is to only come during the season." Rex's second wife, Melonie, had returned even though she hated the isolation of the island in the winter. I hadn't asked Rex exactly why she was staying with him. We weren't really dating so I didn't think it was any of my business.

"You're thinking of a certain sexy cop's second wife, aren't you?"

I put my elbows on the table and rested my chin in my palms. "Yes. Do you know why she came back? All Rex would tell me is that Melonie needed a place to crash while she worked out some problems."

Liz lifted the corner of her mouth in a half smile. "Rex can't help himself from being a knight in shining armor, can he? I heard through the grapevine that Melonie had moved in with an abusive boyfriend."

"Oh no!"

"Well, she had the sense to move out, but then the guy started stalking her and all she could do is get a restraining order against him."

"So she came to Mackinac to stay with Rex because he could keep her safe," I surmised.

"Yeah, I think so."

"Do you think she'll stay with him forever? I mean, how long should you wait for a stalker to lose interest?"

"I heard forever or once they're in jail," Liz said. "Maybe she's hoping he will do something stupid and Rex will arrest him. Once he's in jail, she will be free to live her life."

"Is that fair to Rex?"

"Rex is a big boy," Liz said, and sipped her coffee. "He makes his own choices."

"Yes," I said in total agreement. "He can certainly make his own choices."

"So, how's the repair on the McMurphy going?" Liz asked.

We spent the next hour talking about the McMurphy and the remodel and repair contractors and how I was working with the insurance company to get more money.

My phone dinged and I picked it up to check the screen. "Oh, I have to go," I said. "Maggs just texted that she had some time to talk. I'm going to meet her."

"No worries," Liz said as she picked up the cups. "If I had sat here talking any longer I would have had a second piece of cake. My figure doesn't need a second piece."

I shook my head. Liz had a slender figure and a heart-shaped face with great cheekbones. She didn't have to worry about an extra slice of cake.

Grabbing my coat, I zipped myself back up and tugged on gloves. "Keep me posted if you get any new details?"

"Only if you do the same," she said with a grin.

"I will," I said, and gathered up Mal. "I can't wait to hear what the autopsy results are."

"Me, too," Liz said. "I don't know who would want to kill a twenty-eight-year-old freelance graphic artist, but if it wasn't an accident, I think we're looking at a woman."

"Yes, statistics do say women are more likely to poison than men," I agreed. "But that doesn't mean a man won't poison someone to throw the investigators off the scent."

"Oh, you do think deviously," Liz said as she walked me out. "I like that about you."

I waved good-bye as we left the building and hurried toward the post office, where Maggs had asked to meet me. I entered the building and made the bells jangle. Maggs stood at a counter in the PO box section, writing on a large package.

"Maggs," I said, and greeted her with a kiss on the cheek. Mal jumped up to get a pat on the head. "Why the post office?"

"I didn't want to go to a coffee shop," Maggs said with a shrug. "I've had one cup too many visiting with people today."

"I understand that," I agreed.

"Plus, I have a package that I have to mail so I thought if you didn't mind we could talk here."

"I don't mind at all." The PO box area was on the other side of swinging glass doors and out of earshot of people buying stamps. "How's Frances?"

"She's not talking," Maggs said with a shake of her head. "Something's up when she's not talking to me.

It's only happened one other time and that was when her husband died."

"So she didn't tell you anything about what Rex wanted?"

"Not a thing," Maggs said with concern on her face. "How about you? Have you discovered anything?"

I recounted my meeting with Rex and then my coffee with Liz. "So, Kayla might have been poisoned.'"

"Wow, that sounds terrible. And no one knows why she said Frances's name?"

"I'm not certain the two are connected," I said. "Kayla wasn't asked a question and she only uttered the name. Still, Rex took Frances in to question her late at night. Frances must have been shocked, surprised, and scared. I know I would have been."

"I went to see how she was and cook her breakfast this morning," Maggs said. "She didn't say a word and wouldn't get out of bed."

"You made her breakfast and she still didn't say anything?"

"Yep."

"But last night she said she would tell you everything."

Maggs stuck a label on her package and pushed it through the mail slot. "Let's walk." She put her arm through mine and we walked outside. The sky was still bright and snow melted on the salt-laden sidewalks. There was the crunch of horses dragging sleighs through the streets, the distinct buzz of snowmobiles, and in the distance, children laughing. They must have been outside for recess. "Frances said she was more embarrassed than anything. I don't blame her."

Emotion welled up within me—anger, a touch of disgust, and concern. "This whole thing is nuts. What did the lawyer say?"

"Michael said he advised her to answer with only yes or no and said that they discussed sensitive and personal things that he wouldn't go into."

I frowned. "But you're Frances's best friend. What could they discuss that we don't already know? Frances is the most open and honest person I've ever known."

"I asked her, but she won't tell me." Maggs's mouth became a straight line.

"Do you think she talked to Douglas? Should we ask him what we can do to help?"

"It couldn't hurt," Maggs said.

It was then that Mal stopped me by planting all four legs on the ground. I paused and she turned to sniff a snowbank. Sometimes she would stop me because she had to find a plot of grass, but the snow was piled taller than her and I doubted there would be grass to find. I dug a poo bag out of my pocket in case.

But the dog seemed interested in a person walking quickly toward us. There was something very familiar about her. She was older, probably in her late fifties. Her expression was one of determined rage. She wore a heavy parka and snow boots with jeans. She strode right up to Maggs.

"Maggs Vanderbilt?" she demanded.

"Yes," Maggs said. "Can I help you?"

"Do you know where Frances Wentworth is?" she asked. I noticed that her shoulders seemed to be up around her ears. The chin of her rounded face jutted out and her strangely familiar dark brown eyes glittered. I swear she fairly shook with emotion.

"Why?" Maggs asked, and replied to the onslaught of angry body language by putting her hands on her hips and raising her chin.

"I need to talk to the woman who poisoned my daughter."

"I'm sorry," I said in an attempt to distract this woman and defuse the situation. "Do I know you? You look familiar."

She turned to me and looked me up and down. Her gaze skittered away from Mal. My pup sat beside me and tilted her head as if wondering why the woman was so angry. I wondered, too. "I've never seen you before," she snapped. Then she turned to Maggs. "Where is Frances?"

"You said you think she poisoned your daughter," I said. "Are you Kayla Cramdon's mother?"

"Yes, I'm her mother," Sally Cramdon said, her body language still angry. "And I have a right to confront the woman who murdered my daughter."

"First off," Maggs said, "Frances wouldn't harm a flea let alone your daughter. Second off, I think you should take a deep breath and calm down before you do something rash like accuse a person of murder."

"Who told you that Frances poisoned your daughter?" I asked.

"People were talking about it in the lobby of my hotel," she said. "I went to the police but they refused to give me Frances's address. Then someone told me that Frances owned an apartment in an old Victorian home. I went there but no one answered."

"I live there," I said, and straightened. "Frances is no longer there."

"Then, where is she?" Sally demanded.

"Perhaps you should listen to the police and go back to your hotel," Maggs said with a hint of anger in her voice.

"I don't think you have any idea what you are talking about. If your child was killed and you knew who the killer was, would you go back to your hotel and wait?"

Maggs's face went ashen and she started to shake.

"Ignore her," I said to Maggs, and took her hand in mine. "She doesn't know. Let's just go."

"What don't I know?" Sally called after us when we took a step. "Come back here and talk to me."

"I need to go home," Maggs said to me quietly.

"I'll walk you there," I offered. Mal trailed behind us while Sally pitched a fit. I glanced over my shoulder when things got quiet. She wasn't there any longer. The woman must have decided to find someone else to help her.

"I'm sorry," Maggs said as we approached her home. "I wasn't ready for that. When it comes out of the blue, it hits me like a lightning strike." Maggs had lost her son Anthony in October and while she seemed to be doing pretty well, Sally's question had brought all Maggs's grief to the forefront. I walked her up the steps to the front door.

"May I come in?" I asked. "I can make some tea and Mal and I will keep you company for a while."

Maggs turned to me and patted my hand. "No, thank you," she said. "When the grief hits, I've found it best to be alone for a while and let it just work its way through me for a bit." Her eyes held large tears. "I'm sorry." She said the last in a whisper and gave me a quick hug before unlocking her door and slipping inside.

My heart broke for her. I stepped off her porch and pulled out my phone. I texted Douglas. Ran into Sally Cramdon. She was demanding to know where Frances was. She wanted to confront the woman who poisoned her daughter.

The text showed three dots as he replied. It took a moment. I could see him in my mind's eyes writing how ridiculous it was to accuse Frances of such a thing.

The screen stopped for a moment and then he answered. Thanks.

I didn't know what he meant by that, so I texted Should I let Rex know?

But Douglas didn't answer.

I glanced at Mal, who was busy watering the snow. I had a meeting scheduled with the foreman working on the McMurphy. "Come on, Mal," I said. "Let's take you home."

Walking quickly back to Frances's old apartment I made a mental note to check on Frances afterward. We were supposed to meet this evening for the tree decorating and lighting ceremony. I was pretty sure those plans had changed.

* * *

"All told, I think the repairs to the McMurphy are going well," my general contractor, David Bromley, said. "We have the plumbing inspector scheduled on Monday. The electrical has already passed inspection along with the structural."

David was a sturdy man who stood six feet two inches tall with wide shoulders and narrow hips. He had thinning brown hair and green eyes. I guessed his age was thirty-five. David worked for Anderson Construction. After what happened with my last contractor, I had decided to try a new one. It cost a bit more, but having the top of the McMurphy collapse was reason enough to not hire the same guys. So far, David had been diligent and helpful. I visited daily to inspect the work myself and ensure everything was going to plan.

Truthfully, I didn't know much about construction, but I knew the McMurphy well enough, and after experiencing the last collapse, I knew enough to pay attention when something was not right.

David wore work pants and a blue dress shirt that showed signs that he worked alongside his employees and did what it took to keep the job on track.

"Sounds like things are moving along," I said, and watched the men level the dark wood cabinets as they installed them in the kitchen. "I'm not sure Mr. Devaney will be in today. He and Frances have some personal things to take care of, so call me if anything comes up."

"I will," David said.

I wandered through the renewed space that used to be my apartment. It had taken nearly two weeks to remove all the debris. When my father drew up plans for the rebuild of the fourth floor owner's apartment and office space, I had chosen to keep the office and the apartment separate. That way if I ever moved out of the McMurphy I would be able to rent the apartment out. Not that I had any plans of moving out.

The apartment was simply laid out. From the exterior hallway, you walked into the main living and dining area. In the lower-right corner was a kitchen against the wall with a center bar that jutted out for barstool seating. It gave it a galley feel while still being open. The upper-right corner led to the second bedroom. Behind the kitchen was a short hallway that held a linen closet, the first bedroom, and across from the bedroom and directly behind the kitchen was a compact bathroom with a sink, toilet, and a tub with a showerhead. Those fixtures weren't installed yet. I peeked into the second bedroom and noted the small closet and large window that overlooked the roof of the building next door. The view wasn't that great but it let in a lot of light so I didn't mind spending money on the larger window.

This room was painted pale rose and ready to move in. The linen closet had been rebuilt with fresh wood that was varnished to show off its color. The master bedroom was painted a pale peach. The new windows on the side and back wall let in plenty of light and gave me a view of the alley and the hotel behind us. There was a nice deep closet that ran the length of the bedroom. Across the hall was the still-empty bathroom. I had it painted in pale blue.

The paint tones were all gentle, closer to white than color, and went together well as almost neutrals. The floors were full wood throughout and were currently dusty from the installations. I went back into the living/kitchen area and felt a pang of loss. I had lost all of Grammy Alice and Papa Liam's things. It meant I could make the space my own, but it also meant I had lost the comfort and memories that I gained from Papa's favorite chair.

My phone dinged and I pulled it out. It was a text from Douglas. **Meet us at the light display.**

I texted back with a thumbs-up and with one last look at the workers working on the kitchen, I left the apartment.

The McMurphy was so quiet. The bottom three floors were only mildly damaged when the roof caved in. There was some water damage on the third and second floors but mostly a lot of dust. I had to get them to repaint all the rooms again and clean the carpets. But that was all minor stuff. Now the hotel was empty and the lobby echoed. All the furniture had been pushed to one side so they could check the foundation and refinish the floors and the walls.

I had enclosed the fudge shop in the front-right corner in thick glass walls to keep my pets from harm around hot sugar. Those walls had shattered and needed to be replaced, but the kitchen itself was safe. I needed to get in there and do a thorough scrub on it before I started making fudge and doing demonstrations for the tourists on Main Street.

Outside the light had begun to fade already. The

sun always sets early in the winter months. A crowd had started to gather, bringing out boxes of ornaments and lights for the tree decorating. I glanced at my phone to see if Douglas had left any more messages and ran straight into a wall of muscle.

"Hey, watch where you're going," said a deep voice as a pair of gloved hands kept me from being knocked over.

Embarrassed, I muttered, "Excuse me." Then I noticed that he was a tall man with thick black hair and chocolate brown eyes. He wore a plaid shirt and a tan puffy vest along with jeans and heavy work boots. I closed my gaping mouth, swallowed, and tried to smile. "Sorry, I got caught up in all the Christmas tree excitement."

He grinned and studied me a moment. "Let me guess, you're a fan of Christmas."

"Maybe," I said, and stuck my hands in my pockets so I wouldn't touch him. He was quite handsome. "Or maybe I'm just a klutz."

That made him laugh and the sound of it warmed my skin.

"Well, Christmas klutz, be careful in this holiday crowd."

"I will," I said, and moved through the crowd toward the open lawn. I had to make a conscious effort not to look back over my shoulder. There was something nice in the twinkle of his dark eyes.

"Allie, there you are," Mrs. Tunisian said as she waved me over from the corner of the light festival.

"Hi, Mrs. Tunisian," I said. "I thought you'd be putting the final touches on your light display."

She put her arm through mine and walked with me. "Oh goodness, no need, we finished last night. I'm certain we'll take the grand prize. Now, tell me, how is Frances? Do you have any idea why they brought her in for questioning? I heard that Kayla's final utterance was Frances's name. Is it true? Do you know why?"

I stopped in my tracks. "Mrs. Tunisian, you know if I knew anything I would share . . ."

"Oh, you know something," she said, and gave me the stink eye. "Share!"

"It sounds like you know as much or more than I do. In fact, it seems that I'm always the one coming to you to find out what is going on. Why do you think I know something?"

"Because I heard you were brought in for questioning this morning."

"Well, that's true," I said, and put my hands on my hips, my arms akimbo. "But I wasn't able to give Rex any more insight. Do you know anything?"

"No, dear, no, I wish I could help." She patted me on the arm and grinned. "But, I knew I could count on you to investigate."

"Wait, I never said I was investigating."

She ignored me and walked briskly away.

I headed over to our light display. Douglas was nailing on the final touches.

"Hey, Douglas," I greeted him. He straightened. "What's up? How's Frances?"

"She is not talking to me," he grumbled. "And she's made herself sick over this."

"That doesn't seem like Frances," I said, and frowned.

"It's not and I don't like it."

"Maggs said she wouldn't talk to her about it. We were hoping she at least talked to you," I said.

"Nope."

"Maybe she needs a distraction," I said. "Is she coming to help put the finishing touches on the display?"

"No, she said she has a headache," he said, and turned to pound in another nail. Frankly, I didn't see a need for any more nails, but I think he was expressing his frustration.

"Frances never gets headaches."

"I know," he said, and hit the nail one last time. He blew out a breath. "I can't even talk her into coming out for the lighting ceremony."

"Things are worse than I thought," I said. "I'm going over to your place now."

"Thanks," he said. "Maybe you can talk some sense into her."

Chocolate Sugar Cookies

1 cup butter
1½ cups granulated sugar
2 eggs
½ teaspoon vanilla extract
3 cups all-purpose flour
⅔ cup baking cocoa
½ teaspoon baking powder
¼ teaspoon salt

For the icing:
2 cups powdered sugar
4½ teaspoons meringue powder
¼ teaspoon cream of tartar
3 tablespoons water

In a large bowl cream butter and sugar until smooth. Add eggs one at a time and mix. Then add vanilla. In a medium bowl, mix dry ingredients together. Gradually beat dry ingredients into creamed mixture. Once combined, divide into two balls, wrap in plastic wrap, and chill for 1 hour until firm.

Preheat oven to 350 degrees F. Lightly flour rolling surface with flour or cocoa. Roll out dough to ¼-inch disks and cut into 3-inch Christmas cookie shapes, such as stars. Place on ungreased baking sheets and bake for 8–10 minutes. Remove from pan and let cool on wire racks.

To make the icing, combine powdered sugar, meringue powder, and cream of tartar. Add water 1 tablespoon at a time until desired consistency is reached. Place icing in a decorating bag and pipe designs on completely cooled cookies. Let stand at room temperature until frosting is dry and firm. Enjoy!

Makes 24 medium-to-large cookies

Chapter 6

"Let's go, out of bed," I ordered, and threw back the blankets from Frances's bed.

"No," she said without opening her eyes. She was wearing pajamas and an old robe. "Go away, I have a headache."

"We're not going anywhere," I said, and looked at Maggs, who stood in the doorway and wrung her hands. Maggs had let me in and I had decided to take a firm tack with Frances. It seemed that everyone being kind was only making things worse. "You are getting out of bed and getting dressed for the tree lighting ceremony and for the decoration judging."

"No," Frances said, but less strongly.

"Yes," I said, and pulled on her arm, forcing her to sit up and open her eyes. "Come on. We are not giving anyone anything to gossip about." I pulled her feet to the edge of the bed. She tried to grab the blankets, but Maggs helped me out by pulling them away.

"She's right and you know it," Maggs said. "If you don't come to the ceremony, people will make up all kinds of things about you."

"I don't care." Frances's tone was just above a whisper.

"That's why we're here," I said. "We'll care for you. Now"—I turned to the dresser—"let's get you some nice warm clothes."

"Something festive," Maggs said, and pulled Frances up to a standing position.

I pulled out a lovely Christmas sweater in red, a long wool skirt in dark green, and a pair of leggings and thick wool socks. "Do you need clean underwear?"

Frances gave me the stink eye. "I can pick out my own underwear," she said, and stormed over, grabbed things out of her underwear drawer, yanked the clothes from my hands, and headed toward the bathroom. "I'm taking a shower." Then she slammed the door closed and we heard the shower start.

"I think we made her mad," Maggs said as she stared at the door. "I've never seen Frances mad."

"Better mad than hiding in bed," I said. "At least I hope so anyway." We both chuckled. "Should we wait here?"

"No, she won't go back to bed now," Maggs advised. "Let's go make some tea."

Fifteen minutes later, Frances walked out of her bedroom dressed in proper Christmas spirit. "Let's go." She grabbed her purse, put on her coat and a warm woolen hat, and headed toward the door. We got up quickly, grabbed our coats, and followed her to the boot tray. Frances looked angry and I wondered for a brief moment if I had made a bad decision to bully her.

"The display competition starts in fifteen minutes," I said as I slipped my boots on. Frances opened the door and a blast of arctic air filled the foyer. Then she was gone, walking briskly toward town. I looked at Maggs and she looked at me and we hurried to follow behind Frances.

The streets were filled with people, walking toward the tree lighting or outside checking on their home decorations. Mackinac Island shrunk down to a few thousand in the winter. It certainly made it easier to meet people.

Frances avoided the crowd gathered at the Christmas tree and headed straight for our lighting display. Douglas pounded in the last couple of hooks and was stringing the last bit of lights.

"Well, hello," he said to Frances when he saw her. He went over and gave her a hug. "How are you feeling?"

"I have a headache," she grumbled. "But those two would not let me rest." She pointed at us with her mittened thumb. "So I'm here. What needs to be done?"

Douglas glanced at us over her shoulder. I shrugged and held out my hands, not knowing what to say. Frances didn't get mad or grumpy—ever.

"I have a longer extension cord. I need you to run it over to our electrical outlet and plug it in. We need to see if it works correctly before the judging starts."

Frances grabbed the orange outdoor extension cord and went behind the display to plug it in.

"What did you do?" Douglas whispered.

"We didn't take no for an answer," Maggs whispered back. "I've never seen her this mad."

The lights came on and we stepped back to admire them. We had blinking lights on the carriage wheels. The rest of the display was colored lights outlining the carriage and the horse and the Main Street replica behind them. Each business was outlined in a different colored string. Frances had hand-painted the cutouts so that the display was also lovely in the daytime.

"Wow," I said as I stared at it. "This is better than I thought it might be."

"Oh, Frances, yoo-hoo!"

We all turned to see Mrs. Tunisian and Mrs. Schmidt barreling down upon us. "Oh boy," I muttered under my breath. There really was no place to hide. Maggs went over to stand by Frances, while I stepped forward to block them as best I could. "Hello, Mrs. Tunisian, Mrs. Schmidt," I said brightly. "How is your lighting display coming along?" I made a show of looking at my phone. "The judging starts in five minutes."

"Oh dear, we've been done for ages," Mrs. Schmidt said. Her long gray curls stuck out under a knit cap. Her round face, highlighted by chapped cheeks, proved she had indeed been outside most of the day.

Both ladies wore heavy parkas, snow pants, and thick boots.

"We're going to crush it," Mrs. Tunisian said as she craned her neck to look around me. She seemed laser-focused on Frances. "Frances, so good to see you out. I understand you had a headache. I wanted to bring you some soup, but Douglas said to let you rest." Her bright eyes sparkled with anticipation. "We would love to know what it was like to be interviewed by the police. Is it true what they say?"

"What do they say?" Frances said, and crossed her arms over her chest. Her voice held a tone of caution.

Mrs. Tunisian seemed to be impervious to Frances's mood. "Oh, that your name was the last thing Kayla said before she died. Is it true?"

"I don't know," Frances said. "I wasn't there."

"Any idea why she would say your name?" Mrs. Schmidt asked, her blue eyes sparkling with intrigue.

"I don't know that, either," Frances said.

Douglas stepped beside me between the older women and Frances. "Ladies, Frances is still fighting a headache. She generously came out for the judging." He glanced with meaning at his wristwatch. "Don't you think it's time to get to your display?"

"Oh goodness, no," Mrs. Tunisian said as she pushed through us. "Our display is working and ready. They don't need us there to judge."

"What if the committee has questions?" I asked, trying to dissuade the stubborn woman.

"I'm sure they won't," she said. "Now, Frances, I hope you're going to investigate Kayla's murder. Do you need help? Judith and I are willing to help."

"No one is investigating anything," Douglas said. "Kayla's death was a tragedy and we are going to support her family and the police by letting them conduct any investigation. Am I making myself clear?"

"Oh yes, of course," Judith said, and put her arm through Mrs. Tunisian's. "Come on, let's go await our grand champion ribbon."

Maggs and I turned toward Frances. "Mrs. Tunisian aside, I want to help you. Whoever killed Kayla may use the rumor about her last words to frame you," I said.

"I don't need you to investigate," Frances said, and crossed her arms across her chest. Her parka rustled with the determination of her statement.

"I know you don't need me to," I said. "But I want to do it."

"The answer is a firm no," Frances said, her tone final. "I don't want to speak of this ever again. Have I made myself clear?"

"You have," I said, and felt surprised and hurt by her stubbornness. Frances had never been totally against my investigating before.

The crowd following the judges arrived at our display. They oohed and aahed as the judges looked it over up close and from a few feet away. There were three judges with clipboards and they were marking down the judging criteria.

"Nice work," Mayor Boatman said, and they moved on to the next display.

"When is the announcement of the winners?" I asked as a sudden chill came over me.

Douglas looked at his watch. "Twenty minutes from now," he said. "We should go over to the Christmas tree. The mayor is supposed to speak, then they will light the Christmas tree and announce the prizes in the lighting contest."

"Great," I said. "I'm going to get us all some hot chocolate."

"Make mine with extra marshmallows," Maggs said.

I waved and left them to make my way to a small stand selling hot chocolate, roasted nuts, and candy. The crowd was growing. It seemed that all the residents and some tourists were out tonight to see the tree lighting ceremony. I stood in line and enjoyed the scent of chocolate and roasted nuts. It was a particularly Christmassy smell for me. Growing up, my parents had made a tradition of going out and picking a tree from a tree farm and cutting it down. Then we would stop for hot chocolate and roasted nuts before tying the tree to the top of the minivan and dragging it home.

Michigan was known for its Christmas tree farms and we always had the very best trees. It was hard for us to wait to cut it down. Our family had started out getting a tree two weeks before Christmas, but as I grew up and grew more impatient, I had gotten them to agree that we could get the tree the weekend after Thanksgiving. Ever since it had been tradition to go out and cut the tree on Black Friday and let it rest for twenty-four hours before decorating and lighting the tree the next Sunday.

My heart squeezed a little. I had visited my parents for Thanksgiving, but left on Black Friday to return to oversee the work on the McMurphy Hotel. My mom told me that since I've been gone they bought an artificial tree and put it out the week before Christmas. I guess I could understand why they changed from real trees, but I do love my traditions.

I decided then that I would get a tree for my small apartment. I knew my pets would love it. Finally, I hit the front of the line and ordered the hot chocolates and a bag of roasted and honeyed nuts. They gave me a cup tray with the four medium drinks with lids and I turned and ran smack into a plaid shirt.

"Fancy meeting you here," said the guy I'd run into earlier. "Are you making a habit out of running into me?"

I swallowed my attraction at the sight of his warm gaze. Seriously, I needed to get a love life if I kept being attracted to random strangers. "I could say you are making a habit of getting in my way," I quipped although it came out more surly than flirty.

"I don't mind beautiful women running into me," he said. "Hold on a second." He ordered two hot chocolates and then turned back to me. "I'm Harry Wooston." He stuck out his hand.

I juggled the tray and the bag of nuts to give his hand a quick shake. "Allie McMurphy."

"Nice to meet you, Allie," he said. "Maybe we'll run into each other again soon?"

"Maybe," I said, and shot him a quick smile. Then I crunched my way through the muddled snow to the plowed street and the crowds waiting for the tree lighting ceremony.

"What took so long?" Maggs asked as she picked up her drink, which was marked EXTRA MARSHMALLOWS.

"The line was super long," I said.

"Everyone wants hot chocolate," Douglas deduced as he pulled his and Frances's cups from the tray. "Are those nuts?"

"Yes. They smelled so good, I couldn't help myself," I said. I tucked the paper tray into a nearby recycling bin and went back to my group. The bag of nuts was warm and fragrant and I offered them to my friends. Then I leaned over to Maggs. "How's Frances?"

"Still mad," Maggs said with a shrug.

"What are we going to do?"

"Leave it alone," Frances said.

The heat of a blush rushed over my cheeks. "I hate to see you so upset."

"I'll be fine," she said, and stared at the Christmas tree stage where the mayor was setting up to give her speech. "Just, please, drop it."

I sipped my cocoa and spotted Sandy Everheart in the crowd with her grandmother and her aunts and cousins. I gave her a small wave. She waved back. Sandy had been my assistant and was a chocolatier in her own right. She had been hired away from me by the New Grander Hotel. I didn't mind. She was supporting her sick grandmother and her large family. I couldn't pay her what she was worth. I'd let Sandy work out of my fudge kitchen on her own chocolate business. She made centerpieces and replicas that had drawn a lot of buzz. But the Grander had offered her three times what I paid and much more than what she could make on her own.

I was happy for her, but I missed her. Then I caught sight of Rex. He was in uniform as usual, but there was a beautiful blonde hanging from his arm. It was strange, as Rex didn't usually like to show affection in public while wearing his uniform. He told me once it was because he had spent six years in the army and it was considered unprofessional to show personal displays of affection while in uniform.

Tilting my head to look around a man and get a better view of Rex, I frowned.

"That's Melonie," Liz said as she walked up and caught me staring. I jumped at getting caught and Liz laughed. "Sorry, didn't mean to startle you."

"Well, I certainly can't look innocent now, can I?" I sipped my cocoa to hide the heat of embarrassment in my cheeks.

"They certainly look cozy," Liz said. "I thought you were dating Rex."

"I was until Melonie showed up." That came out sounding more hurt than I meant for it to. "I mean, he did ask if it was all right by me. And Rex can't help it if he likes to rescue women," I said with a sigh.

"Did you want to be rescued?" Liz turned to me with curiosity in her gaze.

"What? No, no, I pride myself on being able to rescue myself," I said, and straightened. "I just didn't know she was going to be here for the winter. I thought they broke up because she hated the winters on the island."

"They did," Liz said. "I'm curious about the whole thing, too."

"Were you two friends?" I asked. "I mean, it's a small island and she was married to a local policeman."

"We knew each other," Liz said with a shrug. "But Melonie was always all about Melonie and when she wasn't then she was all about Rex. There's not a lot of room in there for girlfriends."

"I see."

"If it helps, he doesn't look happy with her hanging on him," Liz said.

Did it help? I wasn't sure. There was a lot going on in my life right now. Worrying about Rex and his ex-wife was the least of my problems. The small high school marching band started in with the song "Santa Claus Is Coming to Town."

Mayor Boatman stepped up to the small dais in front of the decorated tree. "Ladies and gentlemen," she said, and smiled at the crowd. "Thank you for coming out this evening for the annual lighting of the Christmas tree event. We know it's cold out and Becker's Sporting Goods is handing out free hand warmers. For those of you who don't already have a hot beverage, there are several booths in the back selling coffee and cocoa."

"Where's the mulled wine?" someone shouted from the crowd.

The mayor ignored the comment. "This year the Christmas tree lighting ceremony is sponsored by Doud's Market and Ely Smith's Insurance. Be sure and thank these guys when you see them. We'll have one more song by the high school band. Feel free to sing along." She motioned toward the band and clapped as they struck up "O Christmas Tree."

While the band played I caught sight of Sally Cramdon. She seemed to have a full head of steam and moved straight toward Frances. I took a step toward Douglas and touched his arm. He turned to me and I motioned toward Sally with my head. "Sally," I mouthed.

His hazel eyes followed Sally through the crowd for a brief second. Then he took Frances by the elbow and whispered something in her ear before they both pushed toward the edge of the crowd.

"What's going on?" Liz asked me when she noticed how quickly Douglas and Frances left.

"Sally Cramdon," I said, and sipped my cocoa. My heart hurt for Frances. She didn't need a scene right now.

Maggs's mouth became a straight line. "I'll take care of this." Maggs was a sturdy woman and strong for her age. She was also well respected in the community and the crowd parted for her as she cut Sally off two thirds of the way. Words were exchanged, but the band covered most of them. People took notice and a couple of older men I'd seen at the senior center card events flanked Maggs and slowly but carefully walked Sally to the edge of the crowd.

"Should we help?" Liz asked as we both tried to pretend we didn't see what was going on.

"I think Maggs has this," I said. I noticed Rex shrug off Melonie and move toward Maggs. I trusted he would keep this from upsetting the entire ceremony.

The band finished the song and people clapped. Mayor Boatman took the stage. She was a well-dressed woman in her fifties with champagne-colored hair and a sharp chin. She wore a parka and mittens over wool pants and snow boots. "Aren't the kids wonderful?" she asked, and the crowd cheered. "Now for the bit you've all been waiting for. Leslie, can you come up here?" She motioned for Leslie Warrington to make his way up to the dais. "As you all know, Leslie started the tradition of Lights on the Lawn nearly twenty years ago. It has now become one of the most popular traditions of the holiday season. Leslie Warrington, everyone."

The crowd clapped as Les took the microphone. He appeared to be in his early fifties with a short gray beard and sparkling hazel eyes. Les was about six feet tall and neither thin nor fat, simply middle-aged. He was dressed like most of the crowd in a warm coat, jeans, and snow boots. He wore a cowboy hat made of black felt.

"Thank you, Mayor Boatman," Les said as he took the microphone. "Thanks to everyone who participated in this year's Lights on the Lawn. Your entries and the ticketing to view the lights all go toward the new senior center, which opens next week."

The crowd cheered.

"And now the moment you've all been waiting for . . ." Les pulled out an envelope and opened it to reveal a card. "In second place, winner of a red ribbon and two pounds of JoAnne's Fudge is . . . Emery Fastend of Playful Paws Doggie Day Care for his playful pups on parade display!"

The crowd cheered as Emery moved forward to get his prize. I took a moment to look for Sally and Rex, but he must have successfully removed her from the crowd. I couldn't see either of them. I felt as if someone was staring at me and glanced around to see Melonie glaring at me. I didn't know how to react, as we'd never met in person. I sipped my cocoa and pretended not to notice.

"And in first place and winner of a blue ribbon and two tickets to the Christmas ball is . . . Allie McMurphy of the Historic McMurphy Hotel and Fudge Shop with her display of a Victorian Main Street Christmas."

I was stunned and momentarily not sure I heard him right. Liz, clapping and smiling, turned to me. "Go get your award!" She nudged me to the dais.

Picking my way through the smiling and clapping crowd, I stepped up and shook Les's hand, the mayor's hand, and stopped for a photo of me with them both. It felt dreamlike as I exited the stage with an envelope with tickets to the Christmas charity ball and a blue ribbon in hand.

"And the grand-champion ribbon goes to . . . and it's no surprise here, folks . . . Mrs. Tunisian and St. Anne's for their marvelous display, ''Twas the Night Before Christmas.'"

The crowd erupted and I clapped, but also scanned the crowd for Frances and Douglas. They should be here to celebrate our win. But it seemed that Douglas had taken Frances home. Maggs, too, was no longer in the crowd so I made my way back to Liz, who grinned from ear to ear.

"Way to go," she said.

"Thanks, it was a team effort," I said. "I'm sad Douglas and Frances weren't here to celebrate."

"It's probably for the best. Sally looked like she was wanting to make a scene," Liz said as the mayor pulled a child from the crowd to light the Christmas tree.

"She's grieving," I said. "I can't imagine what I would do if I lost a child, let alone discover that child had been murdered."

"I agree. Plus, she doesn't know anyone here so she really has no support group. At least when Maggs lost her son the whole island was there for her."

"You're right," I said. "Maybe there's a way for us to support Sally better."

"How?" Liz asked.

"By finding her daughter's killer."

Chapter 7

The storm started about two a.m. I woke up with the shutters banging on the outside of the house. Mal barked and Mella was having the two a.m. zoomies around the living room. I got up, put on my robe, and looked outside. The wind roared and snow flew sideways. It hit the window like pieces of gravel.

Opening the window brought in a blast of icy polar air. My hair whipped and froze as I struggled to grab the shutters and lock them closed. Then I slammed the window shut and locked it. My face felt frozen and I had a brief fearful thought that I might have gotten frostbite. Sometimes the wind and cold could be so intense that the tiniest exposure would cause frostbite.

"Stupid," I muttered to myself, and hurried through the dining room and kitchen to the bathroom. I turned on the light and ran my hands under warm water. They hurt and I winced as they tingled with the return of blood flow. A glance in the mirror told me my hair was tangled and frozen. Bits of snow melted and dripped onto my bathrobe. My face was bright red and my skin raw.

When feeling was back in my fingers, I dabbed warm water on my face, then rubbed thick cream into my skin. Finally, I carefully combed out my hair and finished just as the power went out. Mal barked and the sound of the wind grew sharp against the back door. "Well, this isn't good."

It took me some moments of feeling my way through the dark kitchen before I found the emergency candles and lit them. I went through the pantry and discovered that Frances had a stash of pillar candles, a lighter, and, even better, an emergency radio. My pets were on edge because of the storm. I lit a candle and carried the rest to the living room, where I started a fire in the fireplace.

It wasn't easy to start a fire in a storm. The wind howled down the chimney, choking me with smoke until I was afraid the smoke detector would go off. Then the kindling lit in earnest and the fire jumped and crackled, knocking back the cold air coming in through the flue.

It was almost three a.m. by the time I had candles lit, the fire roaring, and the radio running. Luckily the batteries were still good.

"Good morning, folks," said the radio announcer. "As you may be able to tell, we've got a pop-up gale in the straits. These kinds of storms produce blizzard conditions and damage. The best you can do is batten down the hatches and wait it out. The Mackinac Island police and fire crews have issued an all-hands alert. They should be the only people out in this weather. The governor has ordered the closing of all roads and airfields. All businesses should remain closed until further notice. This is a big one, folks. Power is reported out across the island. If you have generators, get them going, but remember to keep them free of debris and sheltered from the storm. Do not bring them inside your home or use them inside your home. Carbon monoxide poisoning is a real hazard when using generators improperly. Other hazards include fire from improper use of space heaters. On the opposite end of the spectrum, people have been known to freeze to death. Stay indoors. If possible stay in contact with the elderly to ensure their safety. If you have any emergencies, call nine-one-one. Now, to continue our Christmas selections, here is Bing Crosby singing 'White Christmas.'" The song began to play and I got dressed in long johns, sweatpants, and a thick sweatshirt.

I was back in the kitchen digging through the pantry until I found a tin coffeepot. I rinsed it out, filled it with water, and put it near the fire to heat. The storm raged outside and I debated calling Frances to see how she was doing. It was four a.m. and I doubted anyone was sleeping through this storm. I texted Frances. **Checking in—the power is out but I found the candles and have a fire going in the fireplace.** Then I repeated the text to Liz.

The kettle started to steam and I jumped up to put grounds in my French press coffeemaker, added the hot water, and waited. In the meantime, I dragged a cooler out of the pantry and put everything from my fridge—except the creamer—in the cooler, then put on my coat, hat, gloves, and boots and dragged the cooler out to the frigid back porch. The power might be out but my food would stay fresh in this air.

I came back inside, stripped off my gear, and poured myself a cup of coffee, added a dollop of cream, and took a sip when I heard a crash above me. I jumped. Mal barked and Mella meowed. A second crash followed, I grabbed my flashlight, and opened my apartment door to the foyer. "Is everyone all right?" I shouted in the darkness.

"Who's making all the noise?" Irma Gooseman called from her doorway. I shone my flashlight near her feet to see that she was fine. Dressed in a warm robe, thick slippers, and a hat, Irma looked tired, but okay.

"It's certainly not me," Barbara Vissor called from the upstairs foyer. I shone my light up to see her looking over the balcony. She wore a thick wool cardigan over a flannel nightgown and had on a hunter's cap with the earflaps down. The hallway was cold enough you could see our breath.

I hurried upstairs as best I could in the dark and knocked on Manfred's door. "Mr. Engles, are you okay?" I waited but no sound came from inside. "Manfred?" I knocked again, but still no sound.

"I've got a spare key," Irma said. She hurried into her apartment and came out with a key on a small chain. "We all swapped keys in case of emergencies. Seniors have to look out for each other."

The floorboards creaked as Irma made her way up the stairs. Her flashlight was dull, but adequate. "Are you going in?"

"Manfred's not answering," I said. "I heard two crashes."

"I'll open the door," Irma said, and I stepped aside to let her. She knocked. "Manfred, I'm opening the door!" Then she unlocked it. I shone my flashlight inside. The apartment was set up similarly to mine with the door opening into the main living space. A small galley kitchen was to the left and a single bedroom behind it.

"Mr. Engle?" I called. "Are you okay?"

The apartment was cold. The wind seemed to be coming in through an open window. I assumed it was through the bedroom. The fireplace held no fire. I stepped in and swept the floor with my light.

"Manfred?" Barbara called.

I made my way to the bedroom and sure enough the window had shattered. The icy wind poured in along with gravelly snow. Glass was everywhere. The curtains were sucked in and out by the wind. I made my way carefully through the glass and unlocked and moved the sash up high enough for me to reach out and grab the shutters and close and lock them. It didn't stop the cold, but at least the wind was less fierce. I turned and looked around the room.

There was a double bed in the center of the room. Manfred was in bed and very pale. "Mr. Engle?" I hurried to the side of the bed and touched his skin. It was cold and clammy. He didn't open his eyes. I placed my ear to his chest. His heart was beating but it was very slow and weak.

"Did you find him?" Barbara asked from the doorway. She shone her light at us. "Is he okay?"

"Call nine-one-one," I said. "He has a heartbeat but it's slow and his breathing is shallow and raspy."

"Got it." Irma hurried to the phone on the wall near the kitchen.

"Manfred," I said gently, and shook him. "Mr. Engle, are you okay? Can you hear me?"

There was no response. "Oh, this is not good," Barbara said as she stood in the doorway and held her hand over her mouth. "Is he dead?"

"Not yet," I said. "We need to get him warm. See if you can find any more blankets."

I tucked a pillow gently under his head to lift him up and gently encourage better breathing.

"I found these in his closet," Barbara said, and handed me two blankets. We tucked them around him.

"The EMTs are on their way," Irma said. "It's freezing in here."

"We can't move him," I said, and frowned at the open window. "Do you have anything that can fill that window? Cardboard or something?"

"I have some old pillows," Barbara said. "I'll go get them."

"Great." I searched his end table and found a bottle of pills, but, without knowing what they were for, I didn't want to try to get him to swallow them. "Irma, I have a kettle of hot water on my hearth. Can you grab a pot holder and bring it up? Maybe we can get some tea or something into him."

"Clever girl," Irma said. "If nothing else we could all use a spot of tea. It really is freezing in here."

"Be careful not to let my pets out," I called after her. Then I held Manfred's cold hand and patted it. "It's okay, Manfred," I said. "We're here. Help is on the way."

Barbara rushed in with three old pillows and wedged them between the sash and the shutters. They successfully blocked the cold wind. "Well, that's something, anyway," she said. She made her way to the other side of the bed. "He looks half-dead."

"Barbara," I admonished her.

"Well, he does," she said, and sat down. She picked up his other hand and patted it. "Manfred, don't you die on us. I know you're old and tired, but I need you to stick around, okay? Remember, you were going to fix my garden bed this spring."

He didn't move and that had me worried. "Do you know if he has any health issues?"

"Of course he has health issues, he's seventy-eight years old, for goodness' sake," Barbara snapped.

"Right," I said. "What about his heart? Is he taking nitroglycerin? I'm wondering if there's something we can do while we wait for the EMTs."

"No, he has a great heart," she said. "As far as I know he was only taking cholesterol medicine and something to ease joint damage. Manfred didn't believe in too many prescriptions."

"Okay," I said.

"I have the hot water," Irma said from the doorway.

She wore an oven mitt on both hands and held my tin coffeepot. It was blue lacquered and looked like something you take camping. I was glad to have it. "Your pets are okay, although I might worry about your cat around all those candles."

"I hadn't thought of that," I said with a frown.

"I'll make us all some tea," Irma said. "You go down and take care of those candles then wait for the EMTs. I was told by the lad on the phone that they would be here as quickly as possible."

I looked at Manfred. Even with the extra blankets and the blocked window he didn't look any better.

"It's okay," Barbara said, and put her hand on my arm. "We've got this."

"Okay," I said, and stood. "Holler if you need me." I made my way through the dark center of the house and down the stairs to my apartment. Inside, my place was cozy warm. The candles put off a rich scent of beeswax and citrus. The fire was happily popping and snapping as it danced on the wood in spite of the storm raging outside.

I quickly put out my candles, put a metal grate in front of the fire, and fed my pets breakfast, then I grabbed my jacket and waited in the hall for the ambulance. The minutes ticked away as slowly as hours. Finally, I saw lights flashing through the driving snow. I opened the door and let George and the new male EMT into the foyer. They carried a stretcher and hospital kits. "Thanks for coming in this mess," I said as I pushed the door shut behind them. "It's Manfred Engle. We heard crashes and when he didn't answer his door we went in. Irma had a key." I walked them up the stairs and into the apartment.

The ladies got up and left the small room so the men could work. They had lights that were strapped to their shoulders and they checked vitals. Then they put Manfred on the stretcher and added an IV.

"Any idea how long he was like this?" George asked.

"No," I said. "We only came up when the window crashed open."

"Do you know if he took any prescriptions? Ate anything bad?"

"No," I said, and bit my bottom lip. "I really don't know that much about him. We say hi in the hall and that's about it."

Barbara pushed me gently away from the doorframe. "He was taking a cholesterol drug and some joint medicine."

"What about the drugs on the nightstand?" I asked.

The new guy picked up the bottle. "Looks like sleeping pills. Was he having trouble sleeping?"

"Not that I know of," Barbara said, perplexed. "Irma?"

"He didn't talk to me about anything like that."

"Okay, ladies," George said. "We'll take it from here. I do recommend that you go back to your apartments and stay warm."

"Are you taking him to the clinic?" Irma asked. "Should we go with you?"

"I think the fewer people on the road, the better,"

George said. "I can have the nurse on duty call you with any updates."

"Okay," we all said at the same time. I followed them all out, closing Manfred's door behind us. We watched as George and the new EMT covered Manfred with a blanket and pushed out into the blinding snow to put him in the back of the ambulance. I glanced at my phone. It was now six a.m. and still dark out. We watched from the front windows as the ambulance carefully pulled away.

"What would have happened if the window hadn't been broken?" Barbara said.

"Let's not think about that now," Irma said. "Come on, I'll make us all some tea."

"No, thanks," I said with a soft smile. "I have coffee in the press. It's probably cold by now, but I can heat it near the fire. Any idea how long we'll be without power? I have fudge orders to get out."

"It could be days," Barbara said. "Just depends on how long the storm lasts and then how quickly they can get crews out to the island to work on the lines. I imagine there are downed lines everywhere. It's a big storm. There will probably be damage on both peninsulas as well. You might as well sit tight."

"Thanks," I said. My heart hurt as I struggled not to panic. The storm put a huge kink in my fudge making. I opened my apartment to find the fire was burning low and my pets were glad to see me. I had to wonder, if I'd only gone to Chicago with Trent, I might not be in this current situation.

* * *

The storm still raged at noon. I'd spent the time on the couch curled up with my pets, reading a cozy mystery novel. Frances and Liz had texted me that they were all right. Douglas had a generator so they had power. Frances had asked me to come over and stay a few days once the storm died down enough to go outside. I agreed. I could make fudge from her kitchen in a pinch and satisfy most of my customers. It was going to hurt me to pay overnight shipping on today's batch, but it would be worth it to maintain customer happiness during the holiday season.

At Frances's place I could put a message on my website about the storm and the possibility of back orders. Fingers crossed there wouldn't be that many of them. There was no word about Manfred, but I assumed it was because things were difficult in the storm. Hopefully there weren't too many emergency calls. Most people on the island understood the winter storms and were well prepared.

There was a banging at the front door and I jumped up and hurried to the foyer. Irma opened her door as I looked out the window. Rex stood on the porch. I hurried to open the door and let him inside. Snow swirled in with him.

"Is everyone okay here?" he asked as he took off his hat and wiped his boots on the mat at the door.

"Yes, we're fine," I said.

"I'm fine," Irma said.

Barbara stuck her head over the banister upstairs. "I'm good. Is there word about Manfred?"

Rex's mouth became a straight line. "It's not good," he said. "He's in a coma."

"Oh dear," Barbara said, and clasped her hands to her heart.

"No!" Irma said, and clutched the doorframe.

"Do they have any idea what caused it?" I asked. "Was it the freezing wind from the broken window?"

"I don't know for certain yet, but we suspect he was poisoned."

"What?" We all gasped at the same time.

"Who would do such a thing?" Barbara asked.

"Why?" I asked.

"Manfred is the sweetest person," Irma said.

Rex raised his hand. "Ladies, please. Try to be calm. If you don't mind, I'd like to speak to each one of you separately. I'll start with Mrs. Gooseman."

"Yes, of course," the older women said. I stepped back into my apartment and frowned. This was the second poisoning in three days. Were they connected?

The storm continued to rage outside, banging the leafless trees against the house. The radio crackled and in between Christmas songs spit out reports of snow levels. It was nearly twelve inches deep now. A glance out the window showed it drifting as tall as the front porch. My apartment was cozy from the fire. Mella slept near the hearth and Mal played with her chew toy beside me. It was nearly an hour before the next knock on my door.

Checking the peephole to ensure it was Rex, I opened the door and let him in. Mal greeted him with happy puppy circles. "Come in," I said. "Can I get you some coffee?"

"Is that a camping coffeepot?" he asked as he pulled off his boots, put them in the boot tray by the door, and hung his coat up on the hooks next to the door.

"Yes. I found it in the pantry. Don't worry, I didn't make coffee in it. I have no idea how to make boiled coffee. But it's done a great job of heating water all day and I have a French press."

"Then, yes, I'll take a cup," he said, sounding weary.

"Great." I made the coffee and brought out cream, sugar, and a plate of cookies. "The cream has been in a cooler on the back porch so it's almost frozen."

"You're pretty good at being resourceful," he said.

"My Grammy Alice used to store leftover foods that we refrigerate on the back porch in the winter."

"Yeah, my grandmother also did that. I often wondered how it kept, but it makes sense. The back porches aren't heated and it's well below refrigerator temps out there." He put cream and sugar in his coffee and took a sip. "Ah. First coffee of the day," he said.

"Don't they have a generator at the police station?"

"They do, but I've been out since the power went off."

I handed him the plate of cookies, basically forcing him to take one. "Do you want a sandwich or something?"

"Thanks, but I've gotta get through this inquiry and get back to the station. Things have calmed down a bit since people have adapted to the storm."

"So Manfred wasn't the only emergency?"

"No, we get a few people who don't react well to the initial stress of the storm, then there's the accidents from the idiots who think they are above the weather. The clinic has been full up since about six this morning."

"I thought people here would be used to these kinds of storms. They aren't uncommon."

He chuckled. "That's the problem. They think they've seen it before and can handle it. Anyway, the snowplow has been out since the storm started, trying to keep the main roads cleared for the ambulance."

"Oh goodness," I said. "Tell me you didn't walk here.'"

"No, the windchill is twenty degrees below zero. I have a snowmobile."

"But I didn't hear it."

"Blizzard conditions can muffle sounds," he said, and reached for a second cookie. "Tell me about how you found Manfred."

I related step by step what happened from the power going out to the first crash upstairs. "If the window hadn't shattered, he might be lying upstairs dead." I shuddered at the thought and glanced at the ceiling. "You said he was poisoned?"

"The nurse practitioner at the clinic thought so.

We have samples ready for the lab once the storm breaks."

"Do you think it was the same poison as Kayla?"

"Maybe," he said, and tasted his coffee. "But we won't know for sure until the results come back. I'm taking preliminary statements. I've taped off his apartment. Don't go inside. Once the storm breaks, I'll send Shane and his team in there to search the place for possible poisons. With any luck it will be accidental and have nothing to do with Kayla."

I couldn't let the thought go—stubbornness was my biggest downfall. "If he was poisoned by the same killer, how was he connected to Kayla?"

"I can't speculate," he said, and scratched Mal behind the ears. "I don't think you should, either."

"But could it be connected to the note left on my door? Maybe he saw who put it there and they came back to silence him." I paused. "I don't like the idea that a killer was in the building."

"Neither do your neighbors," he said. "Keep the main door locked for now."

"What did the ladies tell you? Did they see anything? They know Manfred better than I do. I've only lived here since the McMurphy collapsed."

"What do you know of Manfred Engle?" he asked.

"Well, he's in his seventies, but could still get up the stairs to get in and out of his apartment. I think his wife died a few years ago. Irma and Barbara sort of looked after him, but he's not dating anyone that I know about. He likes to spend time at the coffee shop on Main and play snooker with his buddies at the Boar's End bar. As far as I know, he never came home drunk or had any arguments with anybody. He seemed even tempered and put up with the ladies fussing over him. Frances would know him better," I said. "She lived here for nearly twenty years."

"I'll go see her when the storm breaks," he said. The radio on his shoulder crackled and the dispatcher came over with another emergency. Rex stood. "I have to get this. Thanks for the coffee. Sit tight. Keep the front door locked and check on your neighbors."

"I will," I said, and got up with him. He put on his boots and coat and grabbed his hat. "Be careful out in the storm."

"I plan to," he said. "Let me know if you think of anything else."

"Wait," I said when he opened the door. "Will you tell me if his condition changes?"

"He has a sister in Saginaw. I'll give her your number. She can keep you posted."

"Okay," I said, and picked up Mella to keep the cat from going out the door.

"Lock the door behind me," he said, and stepped out into the icy blasting storm and disappeared into the blinding white.

I closed and locked the door and looked up. Barbara and Irma stood in the upstairs landing, looking down at me. "Are you two okay?"

"As okay as two old ladies can be in a blizzard,"

Irma said. "Want to come up? We have sandwiches. We should talk about Manfred."

"Sure thing," I said, and put Mella inside my apartment with Mal and went upstairs. Maybe the ladies could tell me what Manfred's connection to Kayla was and why a killer would want them both dead.

GINGER COOKIE FUDGE

¾ cup sweetened condensed milk
12 ounces white chocolate chips
1 tablespoon ginger
1 teaspoon cinnamon
1 teaspoon nutmeg
½ teaspoon vanilla

Line an 8 x 8-inch pan with foil. Butter the foil.

In a microwave-safe bowl pour the sweetened condensed milk and white chocolate. Microwave on high for 1 minute. Stir. Microwave in 15-second allotments for up to 2 minutes, stirring in between until mixture is smooth. Add the spices and vanilla. Mix. Pour into prepared pan. If desired, cover with sprinkles and chill until set. Cut into 1-inch cubes and serve. Store in airtight container. Enjoy!

Makes 64 pieces of fudge.

Chapter 8

Barbara Vissor's apartment was bigger than mine. It was not only a few feet wider, but held two bedrooms. The second bedroom was tucked behind the public foyer at the front of the house. I guessed it must mirror Irma's apartment since mine and Manfred's were the same footprint.

"More tea?" Barbara asked me.

"No, thanks," I said, and sat back in the striped wing-backed chair. The living area was carpeted and cozy. Barbara had a fire going in the fireplace and her shutters were also closed, lowering the light coming in through the windows, but keeping out the blowing storm. She had a radio playing Christmas music in the background. Her living room was arranged with a low, pastel couch and two chairs upholstered in stripes with a whitewashed wooden coffee table between them. In the corner was a flat-screen TV on top of an antique console television.

Beyond the living area was a dining table with a matching buffet. Then the kitchen. The two bedrooms and bath were located behind the dining area and the kitchen.

"Poison is a woman's murder weapon," Irma said from her place on the couch between sips of her tea. "I didn't think Manfred was the type of man to have women problems."

"He did just dump Phyllis Shrum last week. That woman has a mean streak," Barbara said.

"I didn't know he was seeing anyone," I said.

"Of course he's seeing someone," Irma said. "The man was an eligible bachelor. Don't you know the statistics here? In the sixty-and-older age group on the island, women outnumber men three to one."

"But I thought more men than women lived here," I said. "I mean, it does have a bit of a reputation of being like the Wild West in the winter."

"That's younger men," Barbara said. "At our age most of the retired men move to Florida."

"Why don't you ladies move to Florida?" I had to ask.

"One, my family lives here," Irma answered, touching her index finger. "And two, moving anywhere at my age is too much work!" She touched her middle finger.

"So is dating," Barbara said with a nod.

"Well, that's one thing we can all agree on," I said, and toasted them with my teacup. We all laughed. Barbara had two cats and the orange striped one opened one eye to give us a *keep it down* look. The other slept on the top of the cat tree near the fireplace.

"Did Manfred know Kayla Cramdon?" I asked.

"Maybe," Irma said. "It's a small island and she was a pretty girl."

"Eww," I muttered. "Isn't he in his seventies?"

"Seventy-eight and very spry, I might add," Irma said. "Don't worry, dear. We all like to look at attractive young people. You will, too, one day."

"Never say never, Papa Liam used to say," I said, and sighed as my heart hurt briefly for the loss of my grandfather. It had been less than a year and I still found that memories of him were often accompanied by tiny spears of grief.

"Manfred did like to play snooker at the Golden Goose," Irma said. "Kayla worked there, you know."

"I thought he liked to play at the Boar's End," I said. Had I gotten that detail wrong?

"Oh yes," Barbara said with a smile. "He played at both bars. The man liked to be on the go twenty-four/seven."

"Besides, the Golden Goose had a tournament for the last two weeks. Manfred was there every day. He had bets in the pool for who would win," Irma said.

"Did he win the bet?" I asked.

"He got the second prize," Barbara said. "Ted Compton beat him out."

"So, no one would want to kill him for his bets," I mused.

Irma and Barbara laughed. "Oh dear, no, the man isn't that good at gambling," Irma said.

"He is quite the flirt, though," Barbara said. "I bet he knew Kayla quite well by the time the tournament was over."

"Kayla was poisoned, you know," I pointed out.

"Yes," Irma said. "We put that together."

"Do you think Kayla's killer poisoned Manfred?" Barbara asked.

"I have no idea," I said with a shrug. "But as soon as the storm clears I'm going to find out."

"Well, don't do anything that will get you hurt," Irma said. "We like having you here."

"Yes," Barbara said. "You bring some young energy to the place."

"Speaking of dating," Irma said with a sparkle in her eye. "How's your love life, young lady?"

I choked on my tea and Irma got up to pat me on the back.

"Now, that's certainly a telling reaction," Barbara said firmly. "All right, lady, spill. We've both been there. We might have some good advice for you."

Unsolicited advice wasn't exactly what I wanted at this moment. But it looked like I wasn't going to have a choice.

The storm stopped by six p.m. I went outside and shoveled the walk down to the street. It took me about two hours as the snowbanks had drifted over three feet in some areas. I was sweaty in my polar gear, but didn't dare take it off. The windchill was still well below zero. The night sky was clear and cold and the snow squeaked and crunched under my boots as I labored to finish the drive. The snow-plow drove by once, pushing the street snow onto the sidewalk. That added an extra fifteen minutes to my chore.

The streets were quiet except for a few brave souls like me out shoveling. I heard the sound of a small motor and turned to see a man on a sidewalk plow, plowing the walks beside the street. As he got closer I recognized Harry Wooston.

"Sure, come by now, after I finish our walk," I teased him when he stopped the plow in front of me.

He grinned. "I would have come sooner, but I didn't hear your cries of distress."

I leaned against my shovel handle. "I rarely cry in distress."

"Right, a strong modern woman, then. Just my type."

"You prefer difficult people?"

His grin grew wider. "I do love a good challenge. Let's exchange phone numbers. I happen to have a very nice little plow rig and would be happy to exchange services."

"And what would you want in exchange?" I cocked an eyebrow.

"Dinner," he said, his eyes sparkling in the starlight.

"What if I'm a terrible cook?"

"You're a fudge maker, I highly doubt you are a terrible cook," he said. "But I'll take my chances."

I studied him for a moment. "Fine."

"Good."

I got out my phone and we exchanged numbers.

"Well, then, I've got work to do," he said, and started

up his little plow. "Don't be afraid to give me a call if you're ever in distress."

"I won't." I waved and turned back to the house. A plow would be great for the ladies in the house, I reasoned.

"Who was that handsome lad?" Irma asked when I stepped into the front foyer.

"Harry Wooston," I said. "Do you know him?"

"Ah, the Wooston boy, I heard he was back on the island. I heard he bought an old bed-and-breakfast and is working on fixing it up. His family is from Lansing, you know. They used to come spend the summers.

"Would you move if you had family elsewhere?"

Irma was thoughtful. "Probably." She shrugged. "It can get quite isolated here sometimes and it would be nice to have family nearby. You young people don't think about that now—moving here and there—but family is truly all that matters in this world."

"Where's your family, Irma?"

Tears welled up in her eyes. "I lost my son in Iraq and he had no children." She blinked hard, then smiled. "I'm an only child of an only child. We thought one was enough to bring into the world." Then she patted my hand. "You're young. Take my advice. Two children is not a bad number."

"Thanks," I said, and gave her a quick hug. My phone dinged and I saw a text from Frances. "Gotta go. You have my number if you need anything."

"I do."

* * *

It was eight-thirty p.m. by the time I got to Frances's cottage. I brought my pets because I didn't want to leave a fire going and not be home and I refused to leave them home alone in a cold, dark apartment.

"Come in," Frances said. "I'm just putting dinner on the table."

"Oh my, hope you didn't wait for me." I put Mella down and she took off like a shot under the couch. Then I set down a big box of fudge ingredients and took off Mal's leash and coat. Finally, I wiped the snow balls off her fur before letting her go to find Douglas.

"Oh no, Douglas was out shoveling until I texted you at eight."

"Thanks for that," I said. I took off my boots, coat, and hat and stepped in stocking feet onto her plush living room carpet.

"Of course, with the generator going, you can use the kitchen to make fudge."

"Are you sure it's okay? I mean it might be late before I finish."

"We know, dear," Frances said. "I made up the spare room. You and your pets can stay as long as you need."

I bit my lower lip. "I don't want to put you out. But, you're right, I need to make sure the fudge orders are ready for tomorrow's shipment. What's the weather guy saying? Is the worst of it over? The skies have been clear for almost two hours now."

"Yes, they think it pushed through and the next storm isn't expected until next week sometime."

"Great!"

I stepped into the cozy kitchen decorated with a

red and green apple motif. Frances had put a tiny Christmas tree in the floor-to-ceiling windows of the dining area beside the galley kitchen. The table was covered in a neat white tablecloth and set with Christmas place settings. "Wow, you have the season down."

"I do love Christmas," Frances said. "Wash up and we'll eat. I hope meat loaf is good."

"You know I love your meat loaf," I said, and washed my hands at the sink. Then I pulled up a chair. Douglas came into the kitchen. It was clear he'd just washed and combed his hair.

"Welcome, Allie," he said as he took a seat. "I heard you had quite the day."

Dinner was cozy and fun. I related everything I knew about the storm and the events with Manfred.

"That old fool probably drank some moonshine," Douglas said, and sipped coffee. Frances cut slices of the leftover coconut cake and brought them to the table. "He and Alistair Godfrey are always distilling things to see what they can come up with. I figured he'd poison himself at some point."

"You think that's all it is?" I asked.

"Sure, what else could it be?" he asked.

I played with my cake and realized I didn't want to say it might be connected to Kayla in front of Frances. She was looking better today and I didn't want to spoil it. "I thought it might be a heart problem," I said. "Or a prescription overdose. He had pills by his bed."

"Could be," Frances said, seemingly oblivious to my line of thinking. "It's hard to remember what medicine you've taken or not when you get older.

Doctors are always throwing one pill or another at you. It's especially hard when you live alone."

"I'm glad you both are not living alone anymore," I said, and raised my coffee cup. "Here's to family."

"To family!"

I shooed them out of the kitchen so that I could clean up. After all, Frances had cooked and my mother raised me to wash up. I was glad Frances let me. It allowed me time to prep for fudge making. I taped the paper with the list of orders onto the bottom of Frances's upper cabinet and started working. I knew Frances would keep my pets out of the kitchen while I worked. It was nice to concentrate on something other than the storm and Manfred and Kayla.

About eleven p.m., Frances came in to say good night.

"Do you have everything you need, Allie?" she asked.

"Yes, thanks, this is perfect," I replied. "I do love the view from your kitchen." It was dark out and the windows mostly reflected me working inside, but if you stood close, you could see the street and the Christmas lights in the neighborhood.

"We're still unpacking," she said. "I hope that doesn't bother you."

I glanced at the boxes near the far wall. "Goodness, no, why would it bother me? You have the place decorated so nicely for 'still unpacking.'" I made air quotes with my fingers. "I want to be you when I grow up."

"You are a dear," she said, and gave me a hug and

a kiss on the cheek. "Feel free to let us know if you need anything."

"I will," I said. "Thanks!"

I went back to work producing dark chocolate fudge. I had been able to chop all the extra ingredients such as fruits and nuts in the afternoon, which meant I just needed to make batch after batch of different fudge bases to create the combinations on my order list.

It was about one a.m. when I heard a noise. Mal was sleeping, curled up on a rug by the door. Mella was snuggled on one of the dinette chairs. The sound came again and I turned to see Douglas walking through the kitchen door. He wore pajamas and a robe. "Goodness, you gave me a start."

"Didn't mean to," he grumbled. "Needed some water." He brushed past me as I stirred fudge on the stove. He grabbed a glass from the cupboard, filled it with water, and turned to look at me while he drank. "You think Manfred was poisoned by the same person who poisoned Kayla, don't you?"

Well, that was to the point. "Yes, I thought better than to bring it up in front of Frances. I mean, I don't know what has her so upset about this case, but I respect her enough to . . ."

"Not tell her you're investigating after she said no."

"Exactly," I said, keeping my voice low. "I don't like the idea of her being a person of interest. I don't know why she won't let us defend her."

Douglas was quiet for a moment. "We all have our secrets."

"You think there's something about this that Frances doesn't want us to discover?"

"I think she'll tell us if and when she's ready."

"Okay." I blew out a short breath. "I won't talk about the investigation in front of her."

"I want to know everything you discover," he said. "I can't keep her safe unless I know what's going on."

"I'll keep you in the loop."

"Good. Now, as far as I'm aware, Frances never had any connection to Manfred other than being neighbors. We don't exactly run in the same circles."

"Except, as you mentioned, she lived below him for over twenty years," I pointed out. "Can't help but know your neighbor."

Douglas frowned. "Right."

"I was surprised Rex didn't stop by here to ask questions."

"He called and wanted to, but I said no. No more questions without a lawyer present."

"Okay," I said, and studied the bubbling pot of fudge on the stove in front of me. "That doesn't deter him, you know. He'll ask her to come down to the station."

"I know," Douglas said. "I called Michael. He's going to take her in the morning."

"As far as you know there's no connection between Manfred and Kayla?"

"As far as I can tell," he said. "I've called a few friends. They're going to do some digging. But as of right now the only connection to any of this is the apartment building. First the note that allowed you to find Kayla and then Manfred above you." He paused for two heartbeats. "I think you should stay with us for a while. I want to keep you and Frances safe and it's easier if you're both in the same house."

"I'll think about it," I said, hating the idea of staying with the newlyweds. I liked my own space, but he was right. It might not hurt to have built-in alibis. I'd had trouble with that before. If nothing else I could be closer to Frances if she needed me. "The McMurphy will be ready for guests next week," I said. "So if I do stay it won't be long."

"But it might be long enough," he muttered. "Thanks, Allie."

"Good night," I said as he put the glass down beside the sink and walked back to the bedroom.

Making fudge left a lot of time to contemplate. It usually took at least fifteen minutes for the fudge to come to soft-ball stage. That was a lot of time for my mind to go through all the connections I could find between Manfred and Frances and Kayla. It left me with one thought. Who was next?

Mal and I were out in the morning with Douglas's old sled filled with boxes of fudge. With only three hours of sleep, I was groggy but happy to have two days' worth of orders ready for shipping. Mal was so happy to run ahead as far as her leash would take her and sniff the snow until I pulled her and then let her run ahead again. The main sidewalks were plowed and some people worked on their private walks as we passed. Others, like me, had shoveled the moment the storm ended.

Drifts were up to four feet tall and the white stuff blanketed bushes and gardens and lawns. We passed the light display—the shapes and forms of each display were covered as if someone had come and thrown white sheets over everything. I made a mental note to come back and spend some time fixing our display.

"Good morning, Allie." Mrs. Tunisian waved. She was decked out in parka and mittens, her round cheeks pink from the cold. She and Mrs. Schmidt were already clearing off their light display. "Crazy storm yesterday, wasn't it?"

"Yes," I said. "But I see you're on top of things."

"We want to keep our grand champion ribbon shining," Mrs. Schmidt said as she came around from the back of the display.

"Are they going to shovel a path through the snow for people with tickets?"

"Yes," Mrs. Schmidt said. "The Boy Scouts will be out after school today to make everything look lovely."

"Perfect. Well, I'm off to ship my fudge." I waved and Mal barked and we continued down Main then Market to the shipping office. The bells jangled as I opened the door. I had opted to leave the sled outside, but that meant a few trips in with boxes. "Good morning, Sandy," I said. "I'm glad to see you are open today."

"A little snowstorm is not going to stop us over Christmastime," Sandy said as she took my boxes and began to weigh them. "You're not the only one whose livelihood depends on getting shipments out."

"Right," I said, and Mal happily followed me in and out until we had all the boxes unloaded. "So there are flights today?"

"Yes, they spent about four hours last night clearing the runways. I heard they had some guests who wanted to fly home and others were eager to fly in for the weekend."

"Already, on Friday?"

She shrugged. "Some people like long weekends."

"But over a third of the shops are closed."

"It's the sportsmen, really," she replied as she rang up my bill. "Businessmen like to come up to get away, too."

"Over Christmas?" I don't know why I found that strange.

She shrugged. "I'm neither a high-powered executive nor a sportsman so I wouldn't know. Listen, I heard about Manfred. How's he doing?"

"Last I heard he was in a coma," I said. "They were checking to see if he was poisoned or overdosed on something."

"Overdosing doesn't sound like Manfred," she said. "That old coot didn't like to take pills. He sure could drink everyone under the table, though."

"Strange, there weren't any liquor bottles in his apartment when we found him."

"Maybe he doesn't like to drink alone." She shrugged and finished ringing me up.

I leaned against the counter after I paid with my

card. "Say, do you know if there was a connection be-tween Manfred and Kayla Cramdon?"

"Hmm, no, other than she worked at the Golden Goose and he was a regular at all the bars. How's the investigation going?"

"I'm trying to piece things together."

"You think it's too much of a coincidence that two people were poisoned in two days."

"How often do people get poisoned here?"

"Not that often," she said, and nodded. "I'll let you know if I hear anything. People are in and out of here all day and chat. I might be able to help."

"Thanks," I said. "Come on, Mal."

We made our way to the McMurphy through the back alley and ran into Mr. Beecher. He was a favorite of mine and Mal's. He walked daily and usu-ally took a shortcut through the back alley behind the McMurphy. Today's shortcut was less so since no one plowed alleys. The snow in the alley had drifted two feet high in places and Mal was left to plow through my footsteps. I had been shuffling my feet to make a path for her.

"Good morning, Allie," Mr. Beecher said. He wore a wool coat and fedora and used a walking stick. "Making a path, I see."

"Why are you walking through the alley when the sidewalks are plowed?"

"I like a little adventure," he replied with a twinkle in his eye. Mr. Beecher always reminded me of the snowman from *Rudolph the Red-Nosed Reindeer*. It somehow fit to see him in the snow.

"How have you been feeling?"

"Good, good," he replied. "Got all that sickness out of my system this fall. How's the McMurphy coming?"

"I'm going to find out," I said. "We were on schedule to open next week to try to get some business from the fun run and Christmas. But with yesterday's storm and the power out, I'm not sure if that's still the plan."

"Don't you have a generator?"

"No," I said. "Papa usually closed the place after the season and didn't see a need. I might need to add it to my list of things to invest in."

"Especially since you are selling fudge online." He glanced up at the back of the McMurphy. "It's good to see the old girl put back together."

"Yes," I said. "I think everyone feels that way. Thanks again for helping out with the cleanup and the roof raising."

"You have a lot of friends here, Allie," he said. "Don't forget that."

"It is a small community, isn't it? Say, do you know Manfred Engle?"

"Yes, nice guy, very outgoing, loves to be in the thick of things. Why?"

"He's in the hospital in a coma," I said.

"That's terrible news. What happened?"

"During the storm I heard two crashes above me, so Barbara and Irma and I went to investigate. We found him very sick in bed. The storm had shattered his window. If that hadn't happened, he might have died up there."

"Do they know what caused him to be so sick?"

"Not for sure, but Rex is thinking accidental overdose or poison."

"An overdose doesn't sound like Manfred," Mr. Beecher said. "He brags about not taking too many pills."

"There was a prescription pill bottle by his bedside. I read the name of the drug, but I didn't know what it was for. The EMT's seem to think it was sleeping pills."

"Hmm." Mr. Beecher pursed his lips. "The older you get the more prescriptions the doctors feel you need. Was the bottle empty?"

"No," I said, thinking back. "Do you know anyone who would want to hurt Manfred?"

"The man's a braggart, but most people put up with him as he does have a generous heart. I'm sure Frances can tell you more. How is Frances doing, by the way? I heard she was under investigation in connection with Kayla Cramdon's death."

"She seems okay," I said, and frowned. "She refuses to talk about it and she snaps at me if I mention I want to investigate. But, you see, I can't just sit by while Frances is wrongly accused."

"I didn't think Frances even knew Kayla," Mr. Beecher said. "I told my friends that as well."

"Frances said she only met her once at a town hall meeting. I don't understand why Rex is pursuing this at all. The only link is Kayla saying Frances's name before she died. But they have no idea if Frances Wentworth could have been someone else in Kayla's life and not Frances Wentworth Devaney at all."

"I'm sure Rex knows that," Mr. Beecher said. "Thanks for telling me about Manfred. I'll see if I can visit him. He's at the clinic?"

"Yes," I said. "Take care, and you might find it easier to walk in my footsteps."

"Cheers," he said.

I brushed the snow away from the McMurphy's back door as best I could then unlocked it and went inside. Mal shook off the snow as I stomped my feet on the rug at the back hall. I took off her harness and coat and wiped her feet with the towel nearby then let her go to run like a mad person through the building. The McMurphy smelled like construction— fresh-cut wood, dust, and paint—even on the lobby level, which was not terribly damaged from the collapse. "Hello? Anyone here?" I called.

There wasn't an answer, but I could hear something coming from upstairs. I peeled off my boots and left them by the door to walk through the lobby in stockinged feet. Mal shot up the stairs with me. Construction was going on in the apartment and the doors were open. I walked in to see them putting in countertops. "Wow, I didn't think you would be working today what with the storm and power still being out."

"We need to stay on schedule," David said. "I hope you don't mind—I brought a portable generator. Got it out on your landing right now. We needed it to use the saw to make adjustments to the counter. The daylight helps with the rest."

The countertops I'd chosen were made of PaperStone—recycled paper and nonpetroleum resin. They were durable and sustainable and I thought a great fit for my needs. Plus, they were heat resistant and stain resistant, two things important to a person who worked with hot sugar. I'd chosen a soft tan color to contrast with the dark wood cabinets. The apartment echoed a bit with the work.

"The bathroom is all installed," David said. "Go check it out. We're still on track for you to move in on Monday. Do you have furniture coming?"

"I've got stuff in a storage locker near the airport." I had been ordering things for the last six weeks. Most needed to be assembled, but I thought it best to keep it in the boxes until I was able to move in.

"Cool, let me know if you need help moving stuff. I've got a few buddies who would do it for beer and pizza."

"Thanks," I said, and wandered back to the bathroom. It was indeed ready to go. The new dark wood cabinet with white sink and PaperStone countertop was the perfect size. The bathtub was deep and I'd had a curved curtain rod installed, but I sighed over the loss of the claw-foot tub. A new one would have been too expensive.

"All in all, it's coming together really well," David said.

I jumped at the sound of his voice.

"Sorry, didn't meant to startle you."

"I didn't hear you come up behind me. I guess I was lost in thought."

"The glass for your fudge shop walls is due tomorrow," he said. "We'll be installing it then. I've got the final inspections scheduled for Monday and you'll be good to go."

"Thank you, I know this was a lot of work."

"Not a problem. I like being employed over Christmas. Not too many people needing construction this time of year."

I walked out into the living room and picked Mal up. "Did anything get damaged in the storm?"

"No, the roof is right and tight," he said. "I had a guy go up there this morning and shovel off the top. I'd suggest you do that anytime we get more than four inches of snow."

"I'll let Douglas know."

"Great—oh, and the security guys came by earlier. They have your cameras and detectors and such all installed. We have to wait for the power to come back on. Once that happens they said they'd send a guy out to test everything."

"Perfect," I said. "It's chilly in here, though. Do you have the heat on?"

"I have it set kind of low because we're coming in and out the door." He pointed to the back door, which was partially opened to let in the power cords from the generator that hummed on the back landing.

"Okay," I said. "Everything looks great."

"Oh, hey, I heard you found Manfred close to death yesterday. Too bad, I like the guy. He's always good for a challenging game of snooker."

"You played snooker with him?"

"Of course, most everyone did at one point or the

other. I was in the tournament at the Golden Goose. He whooped us all. I swear he's a hustler. Probably made money at it as a kid. Anyway, that would be my bet if I were a betting man."

"Did he make anyone mad enough to kill him?" I asked.

"Manfred?" David laughed. "Naw, the guy could whoop you and leave you feeling happy you played."

"What about Kayla Cramdon? Did you know her?"

"Nice gal," he said. "My buddy Frank asked her out a couple of times. But she wasn't interested in settling down here. She kept asking questions about Mackinac Island in the 1960s and who was still here from that time, who was in high school, and such. We don't know any of that, of course. Wrong generation. I was in high school in the '00s, you know?"

"Yeah," I said. "I was in high school in 2005."

"Baby."

I laughed at his teasing. "I'll be twenty-nine next year."

"Baby."

"See you tomorrow, David."

"Bring me some fudge next time," he said. "My kids would love some for Christmas."

"Done!"

Mal and I headed downstairs. I got a text from Douglas asking us to meet him at the lighting display. So I bundled Mal and I up and headed out. It occurred to me that Frances might have been in high school in the '60s. Maybe she would have a better idea of why Kayla was asking questions about that time. One thing I did know was that I would have to proceed with caution. It was going to be hard to investigate without Frances knowing. She was smart as a whip and eagle-eyed as well. I would have to tread carefully if I wanted to stay in her good graces.

Chapter 9

"Allie McMurphy?"

I turned at the sound of my name. It was Melonie. "Yes?"

"Melonie Manning," she said, and stuck out her gloved hand. I shook it out of habit. "Do you have time for a cup of coffee?"

"Um, now?"

"Yes, now," she said. Melonie was as pretty up close as she was far away. Her blue eyes sparkled and she looked like a heroine from a Hallmark Christmas movie.

"Well, I was on my way to help Douglas fix our light display."

"I'm sure you can spare fifteen minutes," she said. Mal barked and she took a step back.

"Mal, shush, she's Rex's friend," I scolded my dog, and the pup sat and tilted her head. "Sorry about that. She's really friendly. Okay, I'll text Douglas and let him know I'll be a few minutes."

"Oh, wonderful." Melonie seemed to relax a bit. "Let's go to Lucky Bean."

I let her lead me to Market Street and the coffee shop near the police and administration building. We stepped inside and there was a line.

"Why don't you snag that table by the window?" she said. "I'll buy the coffee. What do you like?"

"An Americano, please, with cream."

"Great," she said. "Anything to eat?"

"No, thanks." I took Mal and made our way through the small shop to the far corner. The tables were bistro style with small metal chairs. I noticed that several of the people in line were cops. They gave Melonie and me the side eye. I had to wonder if she picked this place on purpose.

She brought over two coffees and a single cherry scone and sat down. "Thanks for doing this," she said, and pushed the coffee toward me. "I realized that I've been back with Rex for nearly six weeks and we never talked. The island is too small for us not to get to know each other."

"Okay," I said. "I thought this was urgent."

"Oh, it is." She laughed and touched her throat. "Sort of . . . You see, I want Rex back. I made a terrible mistake leaving the island, leaving him. I want him back."

"I thought you didn't like Mackinac in the winter."

"I was a silly child," she said, and leveled her gaze at me. "I've grown up and I want Rex to know that, to see me as I am now."

"I heard that you came back because you had a stalker?"

"Initially, yes," she said. "But now that I'm here, I

realize how much I miss the place and how much I miss Rex."

"And what does that have to do with me?" I asked as I played with the lid on my cup.

"Everyone knows you and he were sort of dating?" It came out as a question.

"We had a date and it didn't go well," I said. "Mostly we're good friends. I trust him."

"Oh good," she said with dramatic relief. "Then there isn't any unrequited love between you two?"

"And if there was?"

"Well, then, I would be fair and let you know that I'm going after Rex. I've decided to make an all-out campaign to renew our love and get married again." She studied me with a serious gaze. "I will plow through you and anyone else who thinks they can have him. I have the advantage of living in his house, so you won't win. Have I made myself clear?"

I stood, pushing the chair against the wall behind me. "I guess you should be you. Thanks for the coffee." I walked off and she snagged my wrist.

"Most people are surprised about what I'm capable of when I go after something I want," she said low enough for me to hear.

Mal barked and she let go of me. I picked up my dog and walked out. What a strange encounter. I moved with my head down and my dog against my heart. As I passed the police station, I heard my name called. It was Rex. I really didn't want to see him right now. I needed time to process what Melonie said and to understand what I felt about it.

I rushed to the lighting display. When I hit the snow-covered lawn, I put Mal down and made my way through the stomped snow. People were working diligently on their displays, reconnecting lights and standing up displays that had gotten tilted or knocked down in the storm.

"I thought you were going to take longer," Douglas said as he straightened from picking up a nail.

"I wasn't sure," I said. "What do you need me to do?"

"Restring the lights on the end over there." We worked in silence while Mal dug and played in the snow. "Any further information on Manfred?"

"No," I said. "I haven't talked to Rex today. I asked around a bit but the only connection between Manfred and Kayla is the Golden Goose. I haven't been there in ages."

"Trent owns the place," Douglas said.

"You think the Jessops might know something?"

He shrugged. "You can never tell."

"How's Frances? I was worried after I saw Sally about to make a scene last night. I'm glad you were able to get her out of there before anything happened."

"Don't mention that, okay? The whole thing upsets Frances."

I stopped and straightened. "I understand Kayla was asking about what girls were in high school in the '60s. Frances was in high school then, right?"

"That would be about right," Douglas said as he nailed in the last new nail. "I was in Saginaw at the time. Hadn't made it to the island, but Frances was born and raised here."

"Maybe that's why Kayla said her name. Maybe Frances has the answer to a mystery Kayla wanted to solve. She told others she was on the island to look for her family."

"But we know Sally Cramdon is her mom and Sally is from Traverse City, born and raised, as best I can tell."

"What about Kayla's dad?"

"Phillip Cramdon?" Douglas shrugged. "I don't know of any Cramdons on the island back then. Maybe she's looking for Phillip's mom."

"Oh, that could be," I said. "I'll do some digging online and see if I can't figure out who her father's parents were. Somehow this is all connected."

"I'll back you as long as you keep things far away from Frances. Is that a deal?"

"Deal," I said. "The McMurphy will have the final inspections and be move-in ready on Monday. I'm excited to get her back. And David Bromley said we need to shovel the roof when it snows four inches or more."

"Just more work for me," Douglas muttered.

"You love it," I teased, and stepped back to look at the display. "The display looks great again." I pulled the blue ribbon out of my coat pocket and hung it on the top of the cutout. "All we need now is for power to return."

"I heard they'd have it restored by tonight," Douglas said. "Are you coming over for dinner?"

"Sure, and I'll be making tomorrow's fudge there as well. They're going to install the glass walls tomorrow so once they are in place and the power is on, I'll be back to cooking in the McMurphy."

"Exciting times," he grumbled.

I laughed and kissed his cheek. "They are indeed." Next I headed toward my apartment. I needed to gather up ingredients for tonight's fudge making and pick up a change of clothes. I ran into Liz about a block away.

"I heard that you had an encounter with Melonie today," Liz said with a gleam in her eye. "What happened?"

"Is this on the record or off the record?" I teased her.

"I highly doubt anyone wants to read about your love life in the paper," Liz said, and gave me a side squeeze. "But it doesn't mean your friends don't want to know what gives."

"It was the strangest thing. She called my name and insisted I take a moment to get coffee with her."

"Did she say why?"

"She wanted to talk to me."

"And you just went?"

"It was the Lucky Bean," I said, and shrugged. "Nothing devious about that."

"And?"

"And she bought me a coffee."

"And?" Liz's eyes grew wide. "I can't believe I have to drag this information out of you."

"It was strange and I don't know how I feel about the conversation."

"My sources say you walked out of the coffee shop and left your coffee untouched," Liz said. "I think that says a lot about your state of mind. I mean, you leaving perfectly good coffee? Was it Love Potion Number Nine drip?"

"I asked for an Americano," I said.

Liz grabbed my forearms. "Tell me what she said."

"She said she wanted me to know that she fully intends on not only being Rex's second wife, but also his third wife."

"What?"

"Yeah, she's decided she loves him and wants him back and she was letting me know so I could bow out."

"Bow out of what?"

"You know Rex and I were kind of a thing," I said.

"I know. What I want to know is, do you want to bow out?" Liz asked me.

I blew out a breath and kept walking. "I am not a fan of confrontation."

"You could have fooled me." Liz squeezed my arm. "You confront murderers all the time and you make it look easy."

Stopping, I grew serious. "When the McMurphy collapsed, Rex offered to have me move in to his place."

That got Liz's attention. "Now, that's something I didn't know. Why didn't you?"

"Move in with Rex? It was a big step, and I wanted a moment to think about it, and then Melonie showed up and the rest has been awkward ever since."

"I hear Trent is coming back over the Christmas holidays to ensure the Santa run goes off well and to check on the Jessop properties."

"Trent and I aren't on good footing, either." I ran my mittened hand over my face. "I guess I'm bad at relationships. I didn't have a boyfriend growing up and in college I was too busy to do more than go out once or twice. Trent and Rex are the big leagues. I'm not certain I'm ready to play."

"What do you mean?"

"I mean, they're the kind of guys a girl settles down with and I'm not really ready to give up my independence."

"Independence indeshmendence," she said. "Girl, you need to practice having a long-term relationship. Just pick the one you want and tell them that you need to go at your own pace."

"Trent doesn't want to live on the island year-round, and Rex, well, he's had two failed marriages and now Melonie. I just don't think they are the perfect guys for me."

"Honey, nobody is perfect. Mr. Drop Dead Gorgeous No Baggage No Issues Fits into Everything You Think You Want does not exist. Trust me, I've tried that route."

"Oh yeah? And just who are you dating right now?" I asked.

"I happen to be in a steady relationship," she said smugly, and lifted her chin.

"With?"

"Myself." She giggled. "I'm going through a bit of a dry spell. Not a lot of eligible guys on Mackinac and you're hogging two of them."

"Oh, so that's why you want me to pick," I teased. "So you can have the other?"

"Ha!" Liz shook her head. "I dated Rex for two weeks in junior high school, so no, there's nothing there for me."

"And Trent?"

"I'm not a Chicago girl," she said.

"And you're advising me on my love life?"

"Hey, Allie." We both stopped at the sound of a male voice. "You didn't text me."

I turned to see Harry looking very handsome in jeans, snow boots, flannel shirt, and a brown snow vest. "Hi, Harry," I said. "Do you know Liz McElroy?"

"No, I haven't had the pleasure," Harry said, and stuck out his hand. "Nice to meet you, Liz McElroy." He smiled and the skin crinkled at the corners of his eyes with dazzling effect.

"Liz is publisher and reporter at the *Town Crier*," I said proudly.

"Impressive," Harry said.

"You're new here," Liz said with a slight tilt of her head.

"Yes, my first week on the island."

"And you came during the off-season?" she questioned.

"I take it that's not a normal thing," he said, unfazed by the rather intrusive question.

"Most new people arrive in May to catch the best part of the island during their first months," Liz said.

"Mackinac isn't known for attracting large crowds in the winter months," I said.

"Huh, I wouldn't have thought that to be the

case," he said, and his grin widened. I could tell he was kidding.

"Wooston," Liz said. "I don't recognize the last name. Do you have family on the island?"

"My family lived here decades ago, but current family? Not yet," he said.

"Well, aren't you a bit obtuse," Liz said.

I grabbed her arm and pulled her away. "We have to get going. It was nice to see you, Harry."

"It was great seeing you, Allie, and meeting you, Liz. Allie, you have my number. Don't forget to use it."

We walked a full block before Liz spoke. "Okay, how do you know that gorgeous man and why don't I know him?"

"I literally ran into him on Main Street," I said.

"And you gave him your phone number?"

"Not until I saw him the third time and only because he offered to plow the apartment walk," I said.

"Hmmm." She gave me the side eye. "That's suspicious."

"Oh please, not every new person on the island is a killer," I said.

"We'll see about that," she said.

"No wonder you're single," I teased.

We laughed and she walked me back to the condo. "I heard you saved Manfred Engle's life."

"He's in a coma," I said. "They think it was an overdose or poison."

"I was wondering if you think it's related to Kayla's death," Liz said.

"I was worried about that," I said. "But I can't say."

"I get it, you don't want to hurt Frances, but you can tell me what you think."

I stopped as we stood on the front porch. "Off the record?"

"Yes," she said. "But be aware, I'm going to be interviewing the other ladies who live here."

"If they confirm that Manfred was poisoned, then I would bet money it was by the same poison that killed Kayla."

"That's what I thought," Liz said. "And it can't be a mistake that Frances is tied to both victims."

"It's a small island," I said. "Almost everyone on it can be tied to both victims, including me."

"Did you kill Kayla and poison Manfred?"

"What? No!"

Liz nodded. "Neither did I, so how about we work together to figure out who did?"

"I'd love to work with you," I said, "but I'm trying to save Frances and you're trying to sell a story. I don't think we'd make good partners."

Her mouth was set in a thin line. "Fine, but if you figure this out before me, I want an exclusive."

"I suppose an exclusive is the only thing I can promise you," I said.

With the power still out, the chance to get online to do some research was lost. So I gathered up what I needed to make fudge and headed back to Frances's bungalow. I knocked on the door and Mal barked. She always barked when she heard a knock, even if she was outside with me and saw me knock.

Frances moved the curtains to see who was at the door and then let us inside.

"You don't have to knock," she said as she took the two bags of ingredients from me. "In fact, let me give you a key. You should have our spare anyway. It's good if you need to check on us or watch our things the next time we're away."

I took off Mal's jacket, halter, and leash, then pulled out an old towel I'd placed in my pocket to wipe the snow off Mal's feet and legs. "It's your home. I would feel funny not knocking."

Next I took off my boots, stripped off my coat, hat, and gloves and hung them up to dry in the foyer.

"Our home is your home," Frances said as I followed her to the kitchen. Mal and Mella padded behind me on soft feet. "Did you stop and check on the McMurphy?"

"Yes, final inspections are Monday and I can move back in once they are complete. Plus, we can definitely open the doors to let visitors stay for the Christmas holiday festivities."

"That's good news," Frances said. "I know Douglas and I are both looking forward to returning to our jobs."

We put the bags on the kitchen table when the doorbell rang. Mal ran barking for the door.

"Who could that be?" Frances muttered, and went to answer it. I followed behind. Frances peeked out the window, straightened, and took a deep breath. The doorbell rang again.

"Who is it?" I asked, and looked. It was Sally Cramdon. "Do you want me to get it?"

"No!" Frances paused. "No, I'll get it." She opened the door, leaving the storm door closed between them.

Sally was dressed in a thick puffy coat, boots, and jeans. She had a knitted cap on her head and her cheeks were pink from the cold. The sun had started to go down and the sky was a deep blue behind her. I held my breath for a moment, waiting for an outburst.

"Frances Wentworth?" Sally said in a voice filled with emotion.

"Yes," Frances said. "How can I help you?"

"I know why Kayla said your name." Her mouth trembled and her eyes filled with tears. "I'm fifty-four years old and I'm pretty sure you are my mother."

Frances seemed stunned.

"Maybe she should come in," I said quietly. "Is that okay, Frances?"

Frances clutched her throat and nodded. It was as if she didn't know what to think or how to respond. She stepped aside as Sally stepped in.

"Frances, why don't you make some coffee?" I suggested gently to give her some time to get ahold of herself. "I'll show Sally to the couch."

"Okay," Frances said, and hurried to the kitchen.

Mal wanted to jump on Sally and beg for pets, but I pulled her down. "Not now, Mal," I said. "Please come into the living room. I'll hang up your coat."

Sally took off her coat and padded in stocking feet into the living room and took a seat. She looked pale and slightly stricken. "Thank you." She sat on the edge of the couch and studied the room. "This is very well put together."

"Frances has a nice sense of style," I said. "It's warm and cozy." Silence buzzed around us for a moment. I could hear Frances making things in the kitchen. "How are you doing?" I asked Sally. "This must be a lot for you to process."

"I don't know," she said, and her eyes welled with tears. I grabbed a tissue from the holder and handed it to her. She dabbed at her eyes. "Kayla was my everything and at first I thought . . ."

"You thought Frances was her killer."

"Yes," Sally whispered. "Lots of people think so, but then I learned from Kayla's roommate, Ebony, that Kayla was certain she'd found her grandmother."

"Frances?"

"Yes," Sally said. "I was adopted, you see. I was kind of mad about it—you know, my mom giving me up and walking away. I had an okay life, but there are times when you dream that living with your birth parents would have been so much better."

"Did you try to find Frances?"

"I didn't. I was curious, yes. But then I was angry. Especially after I had Kayla. Who gives up their own child? What kind of monster does that?"

Frances paused at the doorway into the living room. "I was sixteen and it would have been a scandal."

I tried to imagine a sixteen-year-old Frances pregnant and giving up the baby. It wasn't what I expected from her. She was always so organized and prepared for anything.

"I'm sorry for thinking of you as a monster," Sally

said as Frances put down a tray with coffee cups, a carafe of coffee, and cream and sugar pots. "I just . . . well, it was hard growing up. My parents loved me, but they were different than me. Everyone else talked about how they were like their mother or their father. I wasn't like them . . . my adopted parents."

Frances poured her a cup of coffee and handed it to her. I noted that the cup shook a bit in the saucer. So I took the carafe away from Frances and poured her a cup and then me.

"I suppose I should have seen this day coming," Frances said. "But the Sisters' charity told me the records were sealed. That I gave up all rights of ever knowing you. Then the charity home for unwed mothers closed in 1975 when the place burned down and as far as I knew so did all the records. I thought it would be impossible after that even with the Internet."

"Kayla was determined," Sally said. "When she decided to do something, she wouldn't stop even if the odds were impossible."

"But how?"

"She learned that I was born in the Sisters' charity home," Sally said. "So she went to the mother house of the order and asked for a list of the Sisters who worked there the year I was born."

"And they gave it to her?" I was amazed.

"No," Sally said. "No, they told her they had lost the records in the fire."

"So then, how?" I asked.

Sally turned her brown gaze on me and I realized the reason she looked so familiar is that she had

Frances's wide brown eyes and oval-shaped face. Her mouth was different, fuller, softer, but it was clear they were related.

"She went to the local hospital and found the doctor who delivered me. He's in his eighties now, but still kicking. He told her that he only knew of where the girls who gave birth that year were from, so she went to each hometown to hunt them down."

"That's how she came to Mackinac," I said. "But why take a job here? Why stay?"

Sally sighed. "She loved it here—the people, the idea that there were no cars. Kayla was a bit of an outdoors person, she loved to snowmobile and hike and bike. The island is perfect for those things. Plus, she was so certain this is where her grandmother was." Sally looked at Frances. "She was digging around in the high school records back in 1965. But then she met you at a town hall meeting and she said our resemblance is uncanny."

"Why didn't she tell me?" Frances asked softly. "If she knew, why didn't she tell me?"

"She wanted to learn more about you," Sally said. "And we were both afraid you would reject us. The morning Kayla died, she was going to meet you. She told me so in a text."

"But we didn't meet," Frances said. "I didn't . . . I didn't know until after—"

I turned to Frances. "Rex told you?"

"He said her phone showed that she had texted her mother and her friends that she was going to meet me. That she was going to tell her grandmother who she was . . ." Tears welled up in Frances's eyes. "But we didn't meet."

"Was it Kayla who left the note on my door? She was on the island. She had to know you and Douglas got married and that you had moved out," I said.

"She told me she was going to leave a note on your door, Allie," Sally said. "She wanted you to go with her to meet with Frances."

"Why?"

"She knew you were part of Frances's circle and you were both the same age, so she thought it would be nice for Frances to have you with her," Sally said. "But then she died." Her voice trembled and she clutched her throat.

Frances reached out to touch her hand and Sally pulled away.

"I thought you killed her," Sally whispered. "I was so enraged. I wanted to see your face when I told you that I knew you killed my baby. I wanted to tell you that you killed your own granddaughter."

Frances had tears rolling down her cheeks. Sally trembled with emotion. I didn't know what to do, what to say except, "Frances didn't do it."

"I don't know if I can believe that," Sally said, and stood. "I came to tell you that killing Kayla won't bury your secret. I have an interview with Liz McElroy in a half an hour. I'm going to tell her everything. The whole world will know your secret." She stood. "If you killed her to keep her quiet, you just sealed your fate."

I stood. "She didn't kill Kayla."

Sally closed her eyes and blew out a long breath. Then she opened her eyes and turned to me. "I waited until I saw you come in, Allie. I wanted someone to be here when I told Frances because she can't shut me up now."

Frances stood when Sally went and tugged on her boots. "Wait, I want to tell you what happened when you were born."

"I don't want to hear it," Sally said. She grabbed her coat off the hook and shoved her arms inside. Mal raced around the room barking at us all. I guess she could feel the thick tension. "If you try to stop me, know that I recorded my story before I came here. I mailed it to a friend and she's to see the press gets it should anything happen to me."

"Sally, wait—" I said.

"Good-bye." Sally walked out, slamming the door behind her.

I was frozen halfway between the door and Frances. The air was thick with emotion and I paused for three heartbeats, took a deep breath, and moved toward Frances. She had fallen back down to the couch, her arms crossed over her stomach as if she was ill. Her face was white.

Hugging her, I sat beside her on the couch as tears rolled down her cheeks and sobs shook her frame. "I'm sorry. What can I do? Should I call Douglas?"

"I'm so ashamed," Frances said, and buried her face in her hands. Her shoulders shook.

"Why?" I asked, and grabbed a tissue, keeping my hand on her back. "Why are you ashamed? Because you had a child in your teens? Because you gave her up?"

She raised her head and took the tissue from me and blew her nose. I grabbed another so she could wipe her eyes. "Here," I said. "Listen, people know you. They love you. We all know what a good and caring person you are. Why would that change?"

"You don't understand," she said. "My generation didn't believe in having children out of wedlock. They most certainly don't forget or forgive that kind of transgression."

I hugged her. "Forget them if they judge you. Every single one of us has made mistakes in our life. You can't think that you are a horrible person for something that happened over fifty years ago."

She wiped her eyes. "Douglas is going to leave me over this, isn't he?"

"I think you know better than that," I said. "Please, you have friends who are standing by you now when the police are considering you as a murder suspect. Trust me, murder is far worse than giving a child up for adoption. Let me call Douglas. You need to talk to him. You need to tell him before he hears it from someone else."

Her shoulders fell and she looked defeated. "I wouldn't blame him if he left. He thought I was a good person."

"You are a good person," I stressed. "I'm going to call him." I grabbed my phone but she stopped me with a hand to my wrist.

"I'll call him." She looked so pale as she picked up her phone. "Douglas? Can you come home? Yes, now, we need to talk." She glanced at me. "Yes, I'm okay. Sally Cramdon was just here. Don't worry, Allie is with me. I just . . . I need you to come home." She hung up the phone and hugged herself. "He's on his way."

"Do you want me to be here when you tell him?"

"No," she said, and shook her head. Mal jumped up to kiss Frances's cheek. She petted her absently.

"I'll stay until he gets here. I'm not leaving you alone."

"Okay," she said. Then covered her mouth. "This is why I didn't want you to investigate. I didn't want you to know. I didn't want Douglas to leave me."

"He won't leave you," I said. "Douglas is made of sterner stuff than that. Besides, it happened when you were just a teenager—a child."

The door opened and Douglas came in, his face grim with concern. "Frances, are you okay?" He quickly yanked off his boots. "What is it?"

I got up and gathered Mal up. "I'll be in the kitchen if you need me."

Douglas sat on the couch and Frances dissolved into tears again. He held her close and my heart squeezed for them. Kayla's death meant that Frances not only had her deepest secret exposed, but she lost a grandchild she didn't even know was alive. How would that make me feel?

EGGNOG FUDGE

2 cups granulated sugar
½ cup butter
¾ cup eggnog
11 ounces white chocolate chips
½ teaspoon nutmeg
1 cup (8 ounces) marshmallow creme
1 teaspoon rum

Line an 8 x 8-inch pan with foil and butter it. In a medium-heavy saucepan combine sugar, butter, and eggnog. Bring to a boil, stirring constantly until it reaches soft-ball stage (around 15 minutes). Remove from heat and add white chocolate chips, stir with a wooden spoon until smooth. Stir in nutmeg, marshmallow creme, and rum. Beat until blended. Pour into prepared pan and chill until set. Cut into 1-inch pieces and enjoy!

Makes 64 pieces of fudge.

Chapter 10

The power came on at about six p.m. and I gathered up my stuff to take it back to the apartment. I'd managed to stay out of the way while Frances told Douglas everything. The tension was palpable.

"I'm heading back to the apartment," I said as I put on my snow boots and coat. "Call me if either of you need anything."

"I'll walk you out," Douglas said, and got up from the couch where they'd both been camped out since he came home.

I gathered up Mal in her coat, halter, and leash, and Mella in her cat carrier. Douglas brought out my bags of ingredients and put them on the sled I used earlier.

"That ought to get you home in one piece," he said, standing on the porch in his stockinged feet. "Text us when you get there. There's a killer on the loose."

I leaned in close. "Will you both be okay?"

"I'm not mad because of something that happened

over fifty years ago," he said. "But I am disappointed that she didn't tell me the minute Rex confronted her."

"I think she held that secret for so long, she didn't feel she could tell anyone. She told me she was afraid of losing you."

"She will never lose me," he said. "She has to trust that. I married her for who she is—warts and all—as they say."

"Maybe now we can all figure out who wanted Kayla dead," I said. "And why poison Manfred . . ."

"One thing at a time," he said. "Go home, settle in, make some fudge. Don't forget to text me when you get home."

"I won't." I waved good-bye and set off with my cat carrier under one arm, Mal by her leash, and the sled dragging along behind.

It was a still, cold night. The stars shone in the sky like brilliant diamonds. The air was crisp with fresh snow and woodsmoke from chimneys. Mal bounced around in and out of the snowbanks along the plowed sidewalk. It would be impossible to get the snow balls out of her fur, but she looked so happy.

The walk to the apartment building was fast and I pulled everything into the foyer and was about to unlock my door when Rex opened the main door. He stepped in with snow on the brim of his hat and his wool uniform coat.

"Hey," I said. "How's Manfred?"

"I'm afraid he died about an hour ago," Rex said, and pulled off his hat and pounded the snow off his boots on the doormat inside the foyer. "I came to let the ladies know."

I winced. "They're going to be so upset. Come see me after?"

"I will. We need to talk."

I opened my door and freed my cat, who went racing off to the bedroom to hide. Then I dragged everything in. Mal tugged on her leash, but I wasn't going to let her go until I could haul her to the bathtub to wash the snow off.

By the time we were all situated, Mal clean and semidry, Mella stalking the tops of the kitchen cabinets for her dinner, and the ingredients put away, it was nearly seven p.m. I stood in stocking feet, fed my pets, and put on a kettle to make tea or coffee. Something warm was needed as my apartment was cold from lack of use and the power being out.

There was a single knock on the door. I peered out to see Rex standing there before letting him inside. "Come in, I was making something warm. Do you want tea or coffee?"

"Coffee," he said with a nod, and took off his boots.

"Have a seat," I said. "Sorry for the cold, but it takes the heater a while to warm the place up once the power has been out so long."

"I'll start a fire in the fireplace," he said.

"Perfect." I made coffee in the French press, added some cookies to a plate, then created a tray with coffee, cookies, cream, and sugar and brought it out. There was a nice fire burning brightly in the fireplace and Rex was sitting on the couch scratching

Mal behind the ears while Mella curled up on the back of the couch near his shoulder. "I thought you might want some cookies."

"Thanks," he said as I poured him coffee and pushed the cream and sugar toward him. "I understand you had coffee with Melonie today."

"It's a small town, isn't it?" I poured cream into my coffee and sat back in the wing-backed chair. "I think she took me to the Lucky Bean on purpose. It was really close to the police station."

"She seems to have an agenda, that's for sure," he said, and ran his hand over his face. "She asked if she could stay for the entire winter."

"You can't kick her out while there's a stalker in her life, can you . . ." It was more statement than question.

"What did she say to you?"

"She asked me if we were dating." I shrugged. "I told her we had one date."

He frowned. "Then what?"

"She said that she had every intention of marrying you again." I sipped my coffee. "I don't think she plans on moving out. She wanted me to stay away from you."

Rex muttered something dark under his breath. "Melonie doesn't speak for me," he said.

"No, but she is in your life," I said. "Now, what do you know about Manfred's death?"

"He was poisoned."

"By the same poison that killed Kayla?" I asked.

"It appears to be the same."

I shifted in my seat. "So the odds are good that they were killed by the same person."

"Yes."

"It's not Frances," I said.

"Frances is a link between both victims," Rex said, and took a swig of his coffee.

"She didn't know Kayla was her granddaughter," I pointed out.

"You know?" He straightened and put his coffee on the table.

"Sally Cramdon came to see Frances. She told us she was going to see Liz for an interview to reveal how Kayla discovered Frances was her grandmother. She said the news was going to blow up the gossip lines on Mackinac."

"She believes Frances killed Kayla to keep her secret quiet."

"I am sure that Frances didn't even know who Kayla was until you told her."

"I agree," he said. "She was shocked when I presented the news to her the other night."

"So why kill a person she doesn't even know? And what would motivate Frances to kill Manfred after living in the apartment beneath him for nearly twenty years?"

"I'm still trying to work that out," Rex said.

"I think someone is trying to frame Frances."

"Why?" he asked. "Why kill Kayla? Why kill Manfred? Why frame Frances? I need a motive for these murders and I need it before another person dies."

"I agree," I said thoughtfully. We sat in silence for

a few moments. "The final inspections on the Mc-Murphy are scheduled for Monday. Then I'm moving back in, and yes, I got the security company to reset up the security. They did it for free because they were unable to prevent the roof collapse."

"Good," Rex said. "That's great."

"How did the ladies take the news of Manfred's death?"

"Irma was distraught and Barbara was quiet. Neither saw anyone unusual coming or going from Manfred's apartment."

"They do like to keep an eye on things," I mused. "So if the killer had been coming and going, chances are one of them would have known."

"We suspect the poison was in the fudge as the contents of his stomach held fudge according to the preliminary autopsy report. I'm having some boxes of fudge we found in his apartment analyzed," Rex said. "If he got it in the mail then maybe we can trace it to the source. But if he picked it up from somewhere, then he might have been a victim but not the target."

"Could Kayla have also eaten poison candy?" I wondered. "If so we need to check all the candy boxes on the island. The killer could have poisoned a whole batch and then put them back on the shelf."

"So the targets would be random and difficult to trace. Then the real victim would be seen as one of many." Rex stood. "I need to get the candy tested and I need to issue a warning about candy bought at the same time or place."

"Ugh, there goes the fudge business right at the peak of the selling season."

"Would you rather people die?" he asked, and he walked over to slip on his boots and coat.

I got up and followed him. "No, I would not rather people die," I said and hugged my waist. "That would be awful and wrong."

"Listen, I'll be careful. I'll double- and triple-check any foodstuff that both victims might have eaten before I put out a warning. But I have to move fast. Others might be poisoned as we speak."

"Take care, Rex," I said as he opened the door.

He glanced at me with a momentary heat in his gaze. "Don't give up on me."

"How about we just live our lives and see what happens?"

He walked out and I locked the door behind him. Then I went to my front windows and watched him stride off the porch and out into the dark night. I had fudge to make and I needed time to process that Frances had a secret before I would let myself moon over Rex.

Let's face it, I didn't like conflict. I wasn't the kind of girl to fight another woman for a man. I preferred men who chased after me. Right now that wasn't Rex.

The next day I had ten boxes of fudge that needed shipping. The shipping office wasn't open on Sunday so I had to make everything and ship it, today, Saturday. That meant I was too busy to dwell on what was happening on the island. I left Mal at home with Mella. The two slept in the warm sunbeam that came through the windows. Manfred was dead and his apartment was an official crime scene so Shane and a small crew had arrived early and spent most of the morning going through the apartment.

It was good to be outside in the cold crisp air. Tourists flocked down Main Street to visit the tree. There was a hut where Santa sat and kids were telling him their Christmas wishes and getting their pictures taken. I had never been a fan of getting my picture taken with Santa. My poor brain kept saying, *Stranger danger.* Luckily my mother was understanding and didn't force the issue. I always wrote my Christmas wishes in a letter and mailed it to the North Pole Sometimes I knew it arrived because Santa brought me what I asked for. Some years it didn't go farther than the Christmas letterbox at the department store. But that didn't mean I didn't believe. I understood that Santa was busy with a whole planet full of kids. Sometimes he messed up. It was only human.

"Allie, wait up!" I turned to see Harry striding toward me.

"Hey, Harry," I said.

"Did you just finish up mailing off the day's fudge?" he asked, eyeing my empty sled.

"Yes," I said. "How's the B and B business?"

"Okay, I guess." He shrugged. "I'm not quite open yet. There's a lot of remodeling work to get done before the season. I'm sure you understand that."

"I do," I said.

"Hey, you have a sled."

I raised my hand that held the rope that was the sled handle. "Observant."

He grinned. "Let's go sledding."

"What?"

"What's Christmas and fresh snow without sledding?" He grabbed the sled rope. "Come on, I dare you to have a little fun."

"Well, if it's a dare . . ." I hurried after him. He strode with purpose to the fort. Kids were climbing the stairs and then sliding down the side of the hill toward the light display. "Oh no, no, no," I said. "We could run into a display and get hurt, or worse, we could knock one down."

"Come on, live a little." He grabbed me by the waist and pulled us both onto the sled and before I could protest further we were racing down the hill. The sheer thrill of it was a joy I hadn't felt in years. We passed laughing kids and landed safely right before we hit the displays.

He got up and reached down for my hand. I gave it to him and let him pull me up. He raised one dark eyebrow. "Want to go again?"

"Yes," I said, and we raced up the stairs. Sledding was a workout and after four or five passes, I was laughing with delight and out of breath from running up the stairs. "Okay, okay," I said between breaths. "I call a time-out."

"But we were just getting started." His brown eyes sparkled and his cheeks were red. He wore a red knit cap with a white pom-pom on the top and I had to admit that I liked sitting on the sled with him, feeling his hands around my waist as we slid down the hill.

"Let's get something warm to drink," I said when I could capture my breath.

"All right," he said, and put his arm around my shoulder. "I'll let you buy me a hot chocolate."

We went to the café off the marina and ordered extra-tall hot chocolates with whipped cream. I would worry about my diet tomorrow. We sat down in the glass window with a view of the straits. Ice had started to form but the water was still warm enough to batter it against the shore. "Do you like being a hotel owner on the island?" he asked me.

I wrapped my hands around the warm cup. "I do," I said. "I love the people and the slower pace. I love the horses and the carriages and, well, everything about it. It makes for a magical Christmas."

"A very Victorian Christmas," he agreed. "I understand the McMurphy is going to reopen again very soon."

"Yes, next week if I have my way about it."

"Will you stay open for the entire winter?"

"I hope so," I said. "We don't have a lot of reservations yet, but I think I might offer a writers' retreat or something to get people to come for the darkest weekends."

"Sure," he said. "Writers like isolated darkness . . ."

"Wow, you make it sound awful," I teased.

"No, that's not what I meant. I meant . . . well, most people vacation in the Caribbean or at least Florida in February and March. Snow and cold and ice are great for Christmas, but after that they sort of lose their enchantment." He sipped his cocoa. "I don't expect any income in the first quarter of the year. So I figure that is the best time to do remodeling work."

"It's also the coldest so it's hard to paint and such," I pointed out. "We have to wait until May to paint the exterior of the McMurphy. Interior paint can also be difficult because you should have windows open and be running your heat."

"But there are contractors looking for work then, right?"

"Yes," I said. "And you may get a better price."

"I might also continue to do the work myself," he said. "I have three months and nothing but time on my hands." He reached out and took my hand across the tabletop. "I'm glad you were spontaneous with me on the sled. It was fun."

"It was fun," I said, and slowly withdrew my hand. "Thanks for thinking about it. I haven't done any sledding since I was ten years old."

"Oh, now, that's a pity. You need to have more fun in your life. I can help with that . . . if you're game."

"Is that a line you use on all the girls?" I teased.

"Only the pretty ones," he said.

I glanced at my phone. "I really need to get back to the McMurphy. Thanks for the fun."

"You have my number," he said as I stood. "Text me. I'm always ready for spontaneous fun."

"I will," I said, "maybe."

"See you later, Allie."

I walked out of the coffee shop, grabbed the sled from where we had tied it up outside, and strode toward the McMurphy. It was fun sledding. I was glad I did it. It helped clear my mind of all that was going on.

The sun was bright at midday and the snow on the sidewalks had melted in patches, revealing the cement below. The light display had only the thinnest of crowds as most people went to see it in the dark. There were Christmas songs playing as I walked down Main Street and I breathed in a sense of wonder. It was as if I'd been transported to a simpler time and place. I did so love the holidays.

"Allie, there you are." I turned to see Mrs. Tunisian and Mrs. Morgan striding toward me.

"Hello, ladies, how are you today?"

"We just came from seeing Frances."

"You did?"

"Yes, after the write-up in the paper's online edition, we thought we would go and let her know we supported her," Mrs. Tunisian said.

"We all make mistakes when we're kids," Mrs. Morgan said. She was a tiny woman with snow-white hair capped with a pale blue knit cap. Her pointy chin and mischievous eyes always reminded me of an elf.

"Still, it was a bit shocking about Frances," Mrs. Tunisian mused. "I am trying to think who the boy might have been." She shrugged. "It was all so long ago."

"I have a question," I said. "You both knew Manfred Engle, right?"

"Yes, dear, it's a small island," Mrs. Tunisian said. "Manfred used to be a dock foreman until he retired twenty years or so ago."

"Do you have any idea why someone would want to kill him?" I asked.

"So it was a confirmed poisoning?" Mrs. Morgan said. "Well, hmmm, no, Manfred was a bit of a nut, but harmless. He was a regular at the senior center as well as the snooker tables."

"Yes, he loved to play in the card tournaments, but he was terrible at it. Never won, not once," Mrs. Tunisian said.

"Rex thinks there's a connection between Manfred's and Kayla's deaths." I pulled the ladies aside to allow a group of fishermen to walk by us. "I understand they both were at the Golden Goose for the last snooker tournament."

"Maybe Kayla saw something she shouldn't have," Mrs. Tunisian said. "If I were you, I'd go see Ralph at the Golden Goose."

"Ralph?" I asked.

"Ralph Finnish is the bartender there," Mrs. Tunisian said. "He might know something."

"So, you're investigating?" Mrs. Morgan asked. "Good, good, you do a great job of bringing these crooks to justice."

"Well, I don't do it alone. Lots of people help me," I said.

"It takes a village," Mrs. Tunisian said. "What can we do?"

"I think we should figure out who Frances's lover was," Mrs. Morgan said.

"Why?" I asked.

"He could be the killer," Mrs. Morgan said. "Besides, I want to know."

"Don't you think Frances has been through enough?" I asked. "If she wanted us to know who the father was she would tell us."

Mrs. Morgan pouted. "I suppose you're right."

"Okay, I've got to move some stuff into the McMurphy. Talk later?" I left to walk to the airport, where I had a small storage unit. I unlocked the unit and opened the door. Inside I'd stored the pieces of furniture I had bought over the last few months to put inside my new apartment. It was safe now for me to start moving them into the McMurphy and putting them together.

I hauled a large flat box with my new bed and balanced it on the sled. Then I added a rectangle box with my new mattress and a smaller box with my new nightstand and finally a lamp. I closed and locked the storage unit and yanked on the sled. It was heavier than I thought it was going to be.

"Need some help with that?"

I glanced over my shoulder to see Patrick Damon. "Hey, Patrick, what brings you here?"

"I have a storage unit for my summer and winter things," he explained, and pointed to a box marked CHRISTMAS TREE. "I came for my Christmas decorations." Patrick was older than me. I would guess he was in his midforties with gray in his blond hair and a scruffy beard that was more like a five-o'clock shadow. "I wish I had thought about bringing a sled."

"I'll share my sled with you if you help me pull it."

"Deal," he said, and put his box on top of the sled and grabbed half the rope. It wasn't too bad once we got started. We stuck to just off the walks so that the sled would move across the snow. Patrick lived just behind the Grand Hotel in a small bungalow that was built for the workers of the Grand. Most of the time these bungalows were empty in the off-season.

"Why do you stay on the island?" I asked.

"A few years back I was promoted to manager and I mentioned to the management that I wanted to live on the island. So they asked me if I would supervise the winter improvements and it went so well, I just sort of kept it up."

"Wow, what a great promotion," I said.

"I do enjoy the island year-round."

"Did you grow up here?"

"I did," he said. "My family has been here for nearly as long as your family. My uncle lived in the Ellsworth cottage."

The Ellsworth cottage was a historic Victorian home that was three stories with a wraparound porch and four to five bedrooms. It was worth over a million dollars. I knew this because Papa Liam loved to talk about all the historic properties on the island and how they were connected to the wealthy families from Detroit and Chicago.

"Okay, now I'm even more curious as to why you are living in a small bungalow and not at the Ellsworth cottage."

He shrugged. "My uncle died a few years ago and

the house is tied up in probate court. I'm not too worried about it as my father taught me I shouldn't count on family money."

"Why?"

"Some sort of nonsense about never knowing when the money will go away," he said. "It's sort of a ritual with the family. We all have to support ourselves until the next person dies and we inherit the money. I guess, I just always saw it as I might be related, but it doesn't mean I'm rich."

"Still, that stinks," I said.

"Crazy, I know, but it's the way it is." He shrugged. "I always figured I might as well do what I want and not worry about an inheritance I may or may not receive."

"That's cool," I said. "Most people don't have an inheritance."

"But you did." He gave me a side eye. "You inherited the McMurphy."

"You're right," I said. "But I also had a choice to sell it. I like the tradition of it, though. So I went to school to learn candy making and hospitality. It was a conscious choice. Besides, my dad made it clear that he didn't want to continue it, and that I wasn't expected to, either. I guess it's nice to make your own choices."

"It is," Patrick said as we stopped next to his bungalow. "I'll take this now. Do you need help getting your stuff home?"

"No, I'm only a block or two away and I think I've got the hang of it."

"See you, Allie."

I waved and with a mighty tug, started the sled back up. It was mostly downhill to the McMurphy and I hauled the boxes through the alley, which wasn't plowed as well, and opened the McMurphy's back door. It was cold and quiet inside. I brought the boxes in one by one and closed and locked the door behind me before taking off my coat and boots. Luckily the McMurphy had an old-fashioned elevator, which meant I didn't have to haul things up four flights of stairs.

My apartment door was unlocked and I opened it to the sight of construction guys packing up for the day. "Hey, David," I said.

"Allie. We're all good to go for now. Just waiting on the inspector's approval on Monday."

"Great," I said as he hurried over and helped me bring the boxes into the apartment.

"Where are these going?" he asked.

"Master bedroom," I said. "I figured I should at least get my bed set up if I'm moving back the day after tomorrow."

"Smart," he said. "Need any help putting things together?" He was studying the picture on the box.

"I think I'm good, thanks," I said.

"Okay, well, have a good night and I'll see you Monday morning about nine."

"Sounds good," I said. I walked the crew out and locked the McMurphy behind them. Then I wandered through the old girl. She was still stately. I loved the creak of her original wood floors. I'd done so much work on her since I had her. First the lobby-floor remodel. Then the second and third floors had been painted and the floors redone. But under the fresh paint and new supports were the bones of this hotel and fudge shop, bones that my ancestors built and cared for. I guess that was my true inheritance.

I put on my boots and coat and opened the door to the alley. A gust of wind and swirling snow pushed the door. There was the dark silhouette in the doorway.

"Allie," I heard Rex say. "We need to talk."

Chapter 11

"Come in," I said. "It's dark out there." Mackinac Island was pretty far north and the sun went down early in the winter. I glanced at my phone. It was six p.m. Rex stepped into the McMurphy and I closed the door behind him. "I was just heading back to the apartment to feed my pets."

"This is important," he said, and took off his hat.

I closed the door. "The kitchen isn't ready so I can't offer you a beverage."

"I don't need a beverage," he said.

"Then why are you here?"

"I'm here to tell you that the lab results came back from Kayla's and Manfred's autopsies," he said.

"On a Saturday?"

"We have to stop all candy production on the island for the foreseeable future," Rex said. "They both had fudge ingredients in their stomachs."

"But it wasn't my fudge," I said.

"We don't know whose fudge it was," he said. "But once word gets out that they were both poisoned with fudge, you won't be selling fudge anyway. I'm going to call inspectors in to inspect every kitchen. Once your kitchen has been released, you can resume fudge production."

"But this is the busiest time of year until the summer season starts. Once the New Year comes everyone will be on a diet and fudge sales historically plummet." I studied him. "I need these sales."

"I have to shut everyone down," he said. "We need to stop this before anyone else dies."

I took a deep breath, my mind racing. I was already behind my yearly goals due to the roof collapse. If I lost fudge sales, I just didn't know how I was going to open for the next season. But how could you argue against preventing a murder?

"Look." He put his hands on my forearms. "I know this messes with your Christmas sales. Frankly, it messes with everyone's Christmas sales."

"What if the fudge was someone's homemade?" I asked. "If you come out to the press that Mackinac Island fudge might be poisonous, you could ruin the island's reputation."

"I know, it's a political nightmare," he said. "I'm going to do my best to keep this under wraps."

"How?" I asked. "And what are you going to do? Test everyone's kitchen ingredients? Do you even know what the poison is? I mean, if you have the poison you can figure out who bought it."

"The lab thinks it's aconite, but that type of poison is nearly impossible to detect in an autopsy," he said.

"So why do they think it's that?"

"They found traces under Manfred's nails along with bits of fudge," Rex said.

"Did they find any fudge packaging?" I asked. "It seems to me that if he ate fudge before he died then there should be packaging somewhere, right?"

"His trash had packages from several fudge shops, including yours," Rex said. "They tested the boxes, but there was no clear winner."

I frowned. "I don't remember selling fudge to Manfred or Kayla. Did Kayla have fudge boxes in her apartment?"

"All I can tell you is that there is a connection," he said. "I've really said too much already. I'm visiting all the island fudge makers personally to let them know we are halting production."

"I don't think you can keep that kind of information under wraps," I said. "How are you going to test all the kitchens? How long will this take? What about the makers who have kitchens in Mackinaw City?"

"We believe this is an island issue," he said.

"So, if I had taken Trent up on his offer and moved to Chicago I would still be able to make fudge to meet my online orders?"

"Yes," he said. His mouth formed a thin line and he let go of me.

I blew out a breath and paced, not sure what to do with this information. "Who's doing the testing? When are they coming? How long will this take? Isn't the crime lab overloaded? You keep telling me this is not like television. Things don't move through the lab in twenty-four or even forty-eight hours."

"I talked to the mayor. We've scheduled for a private firm to come in and inspect each kitchen, take samples, and alert us to any signs of poison."

"This seems ridiculous," I said as I paced. "Who would ruin their business by poisoning their customers? You aren't going to find poison in anyone's kitchen. If the fudge was poisoned, then it wasn't done in a kitchen. Either someone poisoned it in a shop or before they gifted the fudge."

"I have to be responsible and have all the kitchens inspected," he said, his expression firm. "Why don't you take a day or two off and do some Christmas shopping or decorating?"

"Wow, that is a sexist remark."

"Do you think so?" He frowned. "I only meant that you could use the time to do seasonal things."

"Right," I said, and sighed. "When are the inspectors coming?"

"They will be here at ten tomorrow. I've asked them to put you first or second on the list."

"Thanks," I said, then stopped. "Oh, because my fudge box was at the crime scene."

He didn't say anything.

"Fine," I said, and opened the door. "I'll expect them tomorrow. I'm making all my fudge at the apartment." We stepped out into the cold quiet of the evening. My breath came out like a frosty cloud as I locked the door behind us. We walked down the alley toward the apartment. "I've been promised final inspections on the McMurphy on Monday. So I'll be back in the kitchen there making fudge by Tuesday."

"They'll want to check everywhere you're making fudge."

"That's fine," I said. "Is that all?"

"That's it," he said. "Have a good evening, Allie."

"Bye, Rex." We parted ways at the end of the alley. I headed toward the apartment. It had been a few hours and my pets needed dinner. I stepped up to the wraparound porch with the strings of colorful Christmas lights. Someone had put out a blow-up Santa Claus and it waved merrily in the breeze off the lake. I unlocked the main door, then stomped the snow off my boots, and unlocked my apartment door.

Mal rushed me, barking happily. She did her usual slide into me and jumped up as I pulled off my boots and put them in the boot tray by the door. "Hey, Mal," I said as I unzipped my coat. "Anything happen while I was out?"

The pup didn't answer me. She simply wagged her stub tail and bounced up and down. By the time I hung up my coat, Mella was up and rubbing against my leg while Mal continued to bounce. I picked up the pup and reached down to give Mella a scratch behind her ear. "Well, babies, I have a day off from fudge making tomorrow. What shall we do together? Hmm? Rex thinks we should do something Christmassy."

I glanced around the apartment. There wasn't a Christmas decoration in sight. Mostly because the decorations had been destroyed when the roof collapsed and I'd been too busy to think about decorating the apartment. "Maybe we should decorate the McMurphy," I mused, and walked into the kitchen to feed my pets dinner. Once I'd scooped out wet food for the cat and kibble for the pup, I left them to their dinner and went into the living area to light a fire. It was a Saturday night and without fudge to make or a hotel to run, I didn't know what to do with myself.

Picking up my laptop, I sat down and opened it up. My pets came out from the kitchen happy. Mella jumped up on the back of the couch behind me and cleaned her paws. Mal grabbed a chew toy from her pile of toys and sat in front of the fire and chewed contentedly.

Maybe this is what life was all about. Slowing down on a dark December night. Listening to the crackle of the fire with my feet propped up on a footstool. I had opened my laptop to look for Christmas decorations online when there was a knock at my door.

Mal went barking to greet the knocker. Mella leapt up on her cat tree and I pushed my laptop to the couch and got up. "Coming," I called as best I could over the sound of Mal's barking. I scooped her up and checked the peep in my door. Mrs. Tunisian stood on the other side.

"Hi," I said as I opened the door.

"Oh good, Allie, you're here," she said breathlessly. Her coat still had snowflakes clinging to the shoulders as she pushed her way into my place. "How's the investigation going?"

"Not so well," I said. "How did you get inside the foyer?"

"Irma gave me a key to the main door," she said, and looked around. "Are you here alone on a Saturday night?"

"Yes," I said, drawing it out as I wasn't sure it was the correct answer.

"You're too young to be alone on Saturday. What are the men on this island thinking?" She unzipped her coat and pulled off her gloves. "I'm going to have a talk with my grandson. You've met William, right?"

"Was he at a senior center event?" I asked, and winced at how old it made me sound.

"Wow, this is worse than I thought," she said, and shoved her hands in her pockets. "But I'm not here to fix your sad social life, yet . . ."

"Why are you here?" I asked.

"I heard through the grapevine that Manfred was killed by poison candy." Her gaze darted about.

"That's the going theory," I agreed. "You won't find any poison here. I don't even know how to get the kind he was killed with."

"Well, that's where I'm a step ahead of you," she said. "Manfred was killed by aconite made from monkshood or wolfsbane."

"Plants?" I asked. "It's the middle of December and you can clearly see I don't own any houseplants."

"Monkshood is a mountain meadow species, not a houseplant," she said. "I Googled it. Pretty nasty stuff. In the right doses it can kill you immediately."

"But Kayla didn't die immediately," I pointed out, and closed my apartment door.

"Could have been a lower dose or the cold from the snowbank could have slowed the process," Mrs. Tunisian said. "Do you have any tea?"

"Um, sure," I said, and put Mal down. The pup ran over and jumped up on the older woman. "Can I take your coat?"

"I hope it's okay that I invited a few of the ladies

over," she said as she stripped off her parka. There was a knock at the door.

"Sure," I said, taking the parka as Mal raced barking toward the door. She opened the door to Mrs. Schmidt and Mrs. O'Malley, Mrs. Morgan, Betty Olway, Barbara, and Irma.

"Carol!" Mrs. Olway greeted Mrs. Tunisian.

"Betty, come in," Mrs. Tunisian said. "Laura." She waved Mrs. Morgan inside. "Nice of you to come, Mary."

"Good to be here," Mary O'Malley said. " I hope it's okay that I brought Judith." She pointed her thumb at Mrs. Schmidt.

"Of course," Carol Tunisian said. "Allie will take your coats." She made a motion for me to step forward. The ladies piled their coats in my arms and took off their boots. Mella disappeared into the bedroom, but Mal was having a field day with all the attention. I took the mound of coats into the bedroom and laid them on my bed. Lucky for me I was in the habit of making my bed in the morning. What I wasn't in the habit of was having people over at a moment's notice.

"Make yourselves at home," I said as I walked out of the bedroom. I didn't need to have said anything. The ladies had already pulled dining room chairs around the fireplace and facing the couch, where Judith Schmidt had settled in. Mal was in Judith's lap and happy to be garnering attention.

I made my way into the kitchen, where Carol was opening cupboard doors. "The mugs are—"

"To the right of the stove," Carol said. "I know. Everything is where Frances kept it. I'm surprised she didn't take more things with her when she moved in with Douglas." She pulled mugs out of the cupboard and placed them on a tray.

The electric kettle was heating up. I went to the pantry off the back porch and gathered up different types of tea. I had Earl Grey, English breakfast, orange spice, a floral that featured lavender, and then Red Zinger. I brought the teas out to place in a cut glass bowl.

"What, no chamomile?" Carol asked. "Mary O'Malley needs something soothing this time of night."

"I'll go check," I said, and put the teas on the counter and went back to the pantry. I found a chamomile bedtime tea in the very back of the shelf. "What brings you ladies here?"

"I told you, we have ideas on how to help your investigation."

"But it's Saturday night," I protested as I arranged the tea bags in the bowl. The electric kettle flipped off, letting us know the water was ready. I quickly added a sugar and creamer set to the tray of mugs and tea and carried it out into the living room. Carol followed with the electric kettle.

"I heard about the ban on fudge making and figured you didn't have plans tonight," Carol said as she put the kettle down on the coffee table. "So, we're your plans."

"Terrible when a pretty, single young woman like yourself doesn't have a date on a Saturday night,"

Betty said as she pulled a lavender tea bag out of the bowl and plopped it in a purple mug before reaching for the hot water.

"We can fix that," Barbara said. "We know a lot of eligible young men." She waggled her eyebrows at me and then grabbed an Earl Grey tea bag and a brown mug.

"Candace Carrigan's grandson is a good example," Laura said as she handed the kettle to Carol. "He's a doctor."

"I don't need to be set up," I protested, and picked Mal up off the couch. I hugged her until she squeaked and then put her in the bedroom with her favorite toys.

"Oh," Judith exclaimed. "You don't have to lock that sweet pup away."

"She'll be fine," I said. "She has a soft bed and a basket full of toys in there." I grabbed a unicorn mug and a bag of Red Zinger and sat cross-legged on the upholstered ottoman next to the coffee table.

"I just love sharing a cup of tea by the fire," Laura said with a sigh as she wrapped her hands around her mug. "Too bad Frances isn't here. It would be just like it was before she met her beau."

"Just like it was?" I asked.

"We used to meet here once a week," Judith said. "Before Frances got a life." She sipped her tea.

"Officially we were a book club," Carol said. "But we haven't talked about books in years."

"What do you talk about?" I asked.

"Oh, this and that." Carol shrugged.

"Now we talk about murder," Laura said with a

smile. "The crimes on the island got interesting since you arrived."

"You mean since my grandfather died," I said.

"And you arrived and started solving crimes," Carol said.

"We haven't seen you at the new senior center yet," Mary said.

"Shush, she's been busy with rebuilding the Mc-Murphy," Carol said. "Haven't you, dear?"

"And making fudge," I said, and blew on my tea before I took a sip. "I was at the opening of the new center. It seems nice."

"It's pretty fancy with those newfangled coffee machines and the snack bar," Laura said. "Takes all the fun out of bringing in our own dishes."

"You're not supposed to be cooking anyway," Betty pointed out. "You burnt up the microwave in your apartment last week."

"I was baking a potato," Laura said defensively. "It's not my fault that the timer went to thirty when I meant three minutes."

"You got to see that hot new fireman," Judith said. "I heard he's quite the looker."

"What new fireman?" I asked.

"Oooh, you haven't met him yet," Carol said with a bit too much glee. "His name is Mike Hanson and he's been a member of the fire brigade for a couple of weeks. I know his great-aunt, Hilda. I'll see if we can't hook you two up."

"I don't need to be hooked up," I said, and frowned. "I'm perfectly capable of getting my own dates."

"Which is why you are spending your Saturday

night with a bunch of old ladies," Betty pointed out. "We don't need Hilda to introduce you. Laura can explode a bowl of pancake dough. He'll be here in moments."

"I think we've had enough explosions on the island to last me a lifetime," I said.

"Let's talk about Manfred and Kayla's murderer," Carol said. "People don't just mail-order poison like aconite, you know."

"I heard you can get anything off the Internet these days," Judith said, and sipped her tea.

"I don't think they will let you ship hazardous stuff," Laura pointed out. "Remember the postman always asks you if you have anything liquid, fragile, or hazardous in your packages before you mail them?"

"They will still ship the stuff—all you have to do is say no," Carol said.

"But then you're lying to the government," Laura pointed out. "Isn't that illegal?"

"I think it just means the post office isn't liable should someone get hurt," I said. "Mrs. Tunisian—"

"Carol, dear, call me Carol. We talk often enough."

"Fine, Carol, do you have any idea who would use such a deadly poison? I mean who even knows about that kind of thing?" I asked.

"Oh, we all know," Mary said. "The senior center had a whole month of talks by murder mystery people. One of them was by the 'poison guy' who talked to us about all kinds of ways people poisoned people through the ages and how poisons work in murders. He said that authors take some liberties with poisons in their books, but most get it right."

"The poison guy?" Horror tripped through me. They all seemed nonchalant about it.

"Yes, he was quite helpful," Carol said.

"Do you have any cookies or fudge?" Laura asked. "Chocolate would be great with my tea." She raised her mug.

"What you're telling me is that most of the seniors took a class on poisons?" I swallowed hard.

"Sure, we were learning about writing mysteries and such," Judith said. "Not that any of us got very far with the project."

"I thought I saw a box of cookies in the cupboard," Carol said, and stood.

"I'll get them," I said, and motioned for her to sit down. "I'll heat some more water, too." I grabbed the electric kettle and hurried to the kitchen. Certainly if most of the seniors took this poison course, then anyone could have known how to use the poison. But who would actually do it? And most important, why?

I refilled the kettle and set it on its heating element, flipping the on switch. Then, grabbing a box of butter cookies and a package of chocolate sandwich cookies, I arranged them on a plate. I could hear the ladies talking and laughing in the next room and I wondered if I should call Frances.

"Sorry to spring the group on you like this," Carol said from the doorway. "But it seemed you needed our help with the investigation. Betty wants to know if we can go up and see Manfred's crime scene. Irma says they have it taped off, but we all think that maybe you can get us in to see it."

"Why me?"

"Because everyone knows Rex is sweet on you and you're best friends with Shane's girl, Jenn."

The kettle bubbled and the element popped off signaling it was ready. I handed Carol the tray of cookies and picked up the kettle. "I don't think I can get you all into a taped-off crime scene."

We walked out of the kitchen and I noticed Irma Gooseman had joined us. "Hey, Allie, what do you think? Can you get us into the apartment?"

"Hi, Irma, let me get you a mug." I put the kettle down on the coffee table. Irma had pulled up another dining room chair.

"I think she's avoiding the answer," Mary said with an observant tilt of her head. "You know they can't arrest all of us." She stood. "We should go up and take a peek as a group."

"Wait!" I put my hand out as a gesture to try and stop them. "What if there's evidence up there that you contaminate? The killer could go free."

"Honey, the killer is already going free," Irma said. "Besides, my DNA is in there from the night we found him. I'll go."

"I don't think that's a good idea," I protested. "Listen, I have cookies. Let's just talk this through. I'm sure someone here can help me figure out who is putting poison in the fudge."

"They're putting it in fudge?" Laura asked. "That's heinous. We all survive on the fudge industry."

"We have to find who's doing this," Judith said.

"I have my flashlight," Irma said, and pulled it out of the pocket of her sweatshirt. She pulled the hood of her sweatshirt up over her white curls. "Let's go see what we can find."

They all headed for the door. Luckily I was younger and just that much quicker. I stepped in front of the door and shielded it with my body. "No, ladies, no. Let's be thoughtful about this. The police have been through Manfred's apartment and they don't have anything but a few empty fudge boxes. If you cross that line, they will come and arrest you and you will be taking valuable time away from the investigation, just to process you."

"I suppose she's right," Laura said from her position near Carol. She snatched a cookie off the tray Carol held and took a bite. "I heard prison food wasn't all that good anyway."

"She's just afraid," Irma said. "I'm not afraid." She took a step toward me. "I'll video it and bring it back for everyone to review."

"That's a great idea," Carol said, and put down the plate of cookies. She went over to her purse and pulled out a smartphone. "Here, use my phone to record it. Look, it has a flashlight, too!" She flipped on her phone's light and the ladies gathered around to look at it.

I grabbed my phone off the end table, went back to my place in front of the door, and pressed REDIAL on Rex's last call.

"Manning," his voice came across the phone's speaker.

"Is that Officer Manning on the phone?" Carol called.

"Oh, tell him we're going to film the crime scene," Laura said.

"Sheesh, don't tell him that," Irma said, and pushed Laura behind her.

"Allie? What's going on?" Rex said over the phone.

I switched it off speaker and put it to my ear. "Frances's book club is here at the apartment. They want to send Irma into Manfred's apartment to record it so they can see what the crime scene looks like."

"Why would they want to do . . . Tell them not to cross the crime scene tape," he said. "I'll be right there."

"What did he say?" Carol asked.

"I bet he said no," Irma said. "Come on, ladies, let's go before he gets here."

They pushed me aside and rushed into the foyer and up the stairs. I closed my door and leaned against it. Part of me wanted them to get footage of the apartment so that I could look for clues and part of me wanted to give Rex a fighting chance not to have the scene compromised. It made me think, though. I'd bet Kayla's place was no longer a crime scene, especially if her mother was in town going through her things. I made a mental note to try to swing by in the morning. Maybe there was a clue still hanging around.

HOT COCOA FUDGE

2 14-ounce cans sweetened condensed milk
2 cups semisweet chocolate chips
2 packets powdered hot cocoa mix
2 cups white chocolate chips
½ cup mini marshmallows

Line an 8 x 8-inch pan with foil and butter the foil. In a microwave-safe bowl put 1 can of sweetened condensed milk and the chocolate chips. Microwave on high in 30-second intervals. Stir in between until smooth. Add the hot cocoa mix and stir until smooth. Pour into pan. In a second microwave-safe bowl, pour the second can of sweetened condensed milk and the white chocolate chips. Microwave on high in 30-second intervals. Stir until smooth. Pour the white chocolate fudge over the chocolate fudge. Garnish with mini marshmallows. Chill until set. Cut into 1-inch pieces and enjoy!

Makes 64 pieces of fudge.

Chapter 12

Mal and I waited for Rex outside the condo building. I had left my place when I'd heard some crashing in the apartment above and the ladies giggling like schoolgirls who were getting away with doing something wrong. Mal barked when she spotted Rex. He strode up with Officer Charles Brown in tow.

"I wasn't able to stop them," I said as the two policemen climbed the stairs to the porch.

"I didn't think you could," Rex said as he took off his hat and walked into the foyer.

"Thanks for calling, Allie," Charles said, and stopped long enough to give Mal a few pats on the head before following Rex into the building and up the stairs. There was a bit of noise as they escorted the ladies out of Manfred's apartment. Mal and I went inside. I left my door open and reheated the teakettle. I figured the ladies would be back and I wasn't wrong. They trickled back inside, laughing and giggling over how cute the officers were and how fun it was to break the law.

"Teakettle is hot," I said. "And the cookies are

barely touched." Mal jumped up and made herself comfortable on Laura's lap as she settled into my side chair.

"I didn't really go in," Laura said as she poured herself a new cup of tea. "I'm not that much into breaking the law."

"Irma and Carol were the only two to go in," Mary said as she snagged a cookie and took her seat. "But it was fun to imagine."

"What was all the banging?" I asked.

"Carol ran into the dining table, trying to film the scene," Betty said, and picked up a sandwich cookie. "They were both trying to use the phone flashlight. Apparently it isn't as easy to use a flashlight and not disturb a crime scene as they show on TV."

"I never understood why detectives use flashlights anyway," Judith said. "Just flip the light switch. I mean, it's the twenty-first century, for goodness' sake."

"I agree, you can see so much better with the lights on," Mary said. "Certainly filming is easier."

"Breaking into a crime scene is a very serious matter," Charles said as he herded Irma and Carol into my apartment.

"It's trespassing," Rex said as he entered the room.

"Are you going to charge us?" Carol asked.

"He can't," Irma said, and crossed her arms.

"Why not?" I asked.

"I own Manfred's apartment. He rented from me," Irma said. "It's not trespassing. I used my key to get in."

"Huh," I muttered.

"I can't believe you called the cops on us." Irma gave me the eye.

"I didn't want the investigation compromised," I explained. "Don't you want whoever killed Manfred not to go free?"

"We weren't going to compromise the scene," Carol said. "We took a video so we could study the scene without compromising anything."

"Then why were things knocked around?" Rex asked.

"We had an issue with lighting," Irma said, and studied her nails.

"Ladies," Rex began, and put his hands on his hips. "I have removed the crime scene tape. Irma, you may let Manfred's family in to collect his things."

"He didn't have any family left," Irma said.

"Oh, that's sad," Mary said. "What are you going to do with all his stuff?"

"I need to see if he had a will," Irma said.

"You could donate it to a good charity," Betty suggested. "Manfred liked to help people."

"Listen, this is your first and final warning," Rex said sternly. "When I put up crime scene tape, don't cross it. Is that clear?"

"Not even if we own the building?" Carol asked.

"Not even if you own the building," he said. "Next time anyone crosses crime scene tape, I will arrest you and let a judge decide your fate."

"Sounds ominous," Judith whispered to me.

"It is," Rex said. "Have a good night, ladies. Allie, a word?"

I left the ladies as they made fresh tea and talked about their adventure. Charles Brown smiled, tipped his hat, and took off down the porch steps. Rex walked me out to the porch.

"You did the right thing calling me," he said. "I don't think they did any harm, but I don't think we should condone this behavior."

"They may not let me into their club after this," I said as I glanced at the light coming from my window. "No one likes a snitch."

"I haven't heard that term since I was a kid," he said, and the corner of his mouth lifted in a slight smile. That was saying a lot for Rex. I know he worked hard on his poker face when he was in uniform. "You should go inside. It's cold out here. Thanks again for letting me know what's going on."

"I do my best," I said. "You know that."

"I do."

I went inside, closed the door, and braced myself for the ladies.

"Allie, get in here," Carol called my name when I opened the door to the apartment. "We're looking at the video."

They were all gathered around the small cell phone.

"I can't see anything," Judith said. "The screen is too small."

"Send it to me," I said. "I'll bring it up on my computer."

Irma sent me the file and I brought it up on the screen.

"Oh, this is better," Irma said, and studied the video with her reading glasses.

"Manfred was very neat for a bachelor," Laura observed.

"Yes," Barbara said. "He liked to keep things simple."

"We found him in the bedroom," I said. "That's probably the best place to look for clues."

"That part of the video is a tad hurried," Irma said. "You'll see that Rex stopped us. All I could do was a quick sweep of the room."

"It doesn't matter," Betty said. "Now that Rex has removed the crime scene tape, you can go inside in the morning."

"Good point," Irma said.

"Say, Allie," Judith said. "Why don't you have any Christmas decorations up? I put mine up the Friday after Thanksgiving."

"Are you a Christmas Grinch?" Betty asked.

"Oh no," I said, and turned my chair toward the ladies. "What with everything going on, I just haven't had time. Besides, I'm hoping to move back to the McMurphy come Monday."

"Oh, we're going to miss you," Irma said. "It was fun to have young energy in the building."

"I still think you should get a tree for this apartment," Laura said. "I have a tree in every room."

"Now, that's overkill," Carol said.

"All right, ladies, I think we've taken up enough of Allie's time. She needs to make fudge in the morning," Irma said.

I started to say that fudge making was on hold for a day or two, but bit my lip instead.

"Plus, the cookies are all gone," Mary said.

"Well, Allie." Laura stood. "If you need any help finding or decorating your Christmas tree, you just let me know. I've got all kinds of ornaments and some great ideas for a tree to fit this decor."

"Thanks, I will," I said, stood, and gathered cups onto the tray as the ladies put on their coats and boots.

"I'll see everyone out," Irma said.

"Have a good night." I took the tray into the kitchen. I heard the door close and quiet descended as I started a sink full of soapy water to wash the dishes.

"That was mighty nice of you to let us invade you like that," Irma said, and came into the kitchen. She grabbed an apron and tied it around her thick waist. "I'll wash. You dry, since you know where to put things."

"Wonderful." I pulled a clean towel from the towel drawer. "I'm sorry for ruining your fun, but you had to know that I had to call Rex."

"It's okay," Irma said as she washed and rinsed the teacups and put them in the dish drainer. "Making the video was just a bit of entertainment for the ladies. I didn't expect to find anything."

"Have you talked to Frances?" I asked. "I've been trying to give her a little space."

"Me, too," Irma said. "But let me tell you, when you find out who killed Manfred and that poor girl, I'm going to give them a piece of my mind."

"Do you have any idea who it might be?" I asked.

"I've given it some thought," she said. "I think the

key is Frances. She knows something that will help the case."

"But I can't ask her," I said. "You didn't see her face when she told us about her secret. She was devastated. Although, I don't know why."

"Oh, honey, you have no idea what it's like to be a pregnant teen," Irma said. "Especially when we were young. Not that I know firsthand, but I can imagine what she went through. Birth control pills were a brand-new thing and don't even get me started on condoms. We were not part of the so-called sexual revolution. We were all good girls who waited until we got married or were considered horrible if anyone found out we didn't wait. Don't forget, Frances wanted to be a teacher. Teachers are held to even higher standards in the community. They are supposed to be shining examples for everyone. Why, I don't think she would have been able to be a teacher if anyone had found out that she had had a child as a teenager."

"That's crazy," I said. "Everybody makes mistakes."

"Having sex outside of marriage was not a mistake people in our generation made. Oh, it was done, but not by good girls," Irma said. "Unless you were trying to get your man to marry you, of course."

"You don't think Manfred was the father, do you?" I mused.

"Why on earth would you say that?" Irma turned to stare at me as if I had just grown a second head.

I shrugged. "I'm trying to connect the dots."

Irma laughed. "Oh, honey, I don't think so. Manfred was never the boyfriend type. Trust me, if anything had been going on between him and Frances over the years, I would have known. Why, they barely talked to one another beyond the occasional hello."

"Doesn't that seem odd?" I pressed, and dried the last teacup. "Frances talks to everyone as if they are her family, and in a way, we all are, aren't we?"

"It wasn't Frances who was standoffish," Irma said. "You know that. How many times did you talk with Manfred?"

I thought about it. "I said hello whenever I saw him."

"And did he engage in any type of conversation with you?"

"No," I said, and frowned. "Come to think of it, he didn't. I guess I just put it down to him wanting to not be bothered by people. Some people are like that, you know."

"I do know and that's my point," Irma said. "The man didn't even have any family. I don't know what I'm going to do with all of his things."

"It was a good idea to donate them. I heard there's a community warehouse that takes household things— even mattresses to give to homeless people who are getting back on their feet."

"Well, now, that sounds like something I should look into," Irma said.

"You know, Mrs. Tunisian . . . er, Carol, suggested that the poison that killed Kayla and Manfred could be ordered online. Do you think that's how the killer got it?"

"Only if they wanted to be caught," Irma said. "I hear all the time about the so-called dark Web, but, honey, if they get a warrant for your computer they can see everywhere you search."

"Let's say our killer is smart," I said. "How else would you get that poison?"

"Well, if they're smart then they are playing the long game."

"What do you mean?" I turned and leaned against the cupboard.

"They have been planning this kill for months, even years. Let's say they have, then they could have brought the monkshood plant on the island and are growing it in their home or greenhouse. They may have created the poison themselves and maybe even experimented with proper dosing by killing small animals."

"Oh, that's gruesome," I said with a frown. "Poison is usually a woman's way of killing. I just can't see a woman killing small animals."

"Honey, we do it all the time when we put rat poison out."

"Doesn't mean we like it."

"You asked what I thought," she said with a shrug, and let the water out of the sink. "Or they could have gotten it from a trip off the island for the express purpose of killing Kayla and Manfred. Who knows? I doubt there would be a way of finding out."

"You're right," I said with a sigh. "I must be tired."

"Oh, I do have something that might help you," she said. "I'll be right back." Irma left my apartment so I went to the bedroom to let my pets out.

Mella was asleep on top of the bed. Mal was curled up in her doggie bed next to her toys. The pup jumped up and came to greet me. I picked her up and brought her into the living area in front of the fire with me.

"Knock, knock," Irma said.

"Come on in," I replied as the door was open. She stepped inside the apartment and closed the door behind her.

"I remembered I had yearbooks from when I was in high school. Frances was in the grade below me, so I don't have her senior year, but I do have the others." Irma sat down on the couch beside me and opened the first book. "Gosh, I haven't looked at these in decades."

"I can't believe you were able to find them so quickly," I said. "I have no idea where my yearbooks are . . . maybe in my mom's attic."

"Well, you see, I don't have an attic and I cleaned out my mother's house years ago when she died. I put these on a bookshelf in my bedroom. I was considering donating them to the local historic society, but I imagine they already have copies." She opened the pages and I was treated to photos from the 1960s of the small Mackinac Island high school classes. "Look, here I am and that's Frances." She pointed to two young women in dresses with petticoats and cat-eyed glasses. "We were on the yearbook committee together her freshman year."

We thumbed through the pages. I was fascinated with the clothes and the school. "The current school building was built in 1969 after we graduated," Irma said. "We went to school in the Indian Dormitory, where the current art museum is."

"That's so interesting," I said. "Were all the grades in that building?"

"Yes," Irma said. "There weren't that many of us who stayed on the island year-round."

"So, then surely you know who Frances's boyfriend was . . ."

"There certainly weren't that many boys to choose from," Irma said thoughtfully as she turned the pages. "I have to assume it was a boy and not a grown man."

"Oh, let's hope so."

"Well, men married younger girls back in our day. Most girls didn't even finish high school."

"Wow," I said, and studied the pictures. "It certainly was a different time. Do you think it was Frances's first husband?"

Irma looked up at me. "I sincerely doubt it, dear. If it was her Richard, then she would have most likely married him and kept the child. Don't you think?"

"Oh, that's true," I said. "What if it was one of the vacationer's sons? That would make more sense, right? I mean, he would be long gone once she discovered her dilemma. Gosh, I wish we could ask Frances about it straight out."

"You should go see her tomorrow and see how she's doing," Irma said. She stood. "I've taken up enough of your night. Would you like to keep the yearbooks for a few days?"

"Yes," I said. "Thank you!"

"You're welcome," Irma said, and then covered a yawn. "Well, bedtime for me. I will talk to you tomorrow."

"Good night, Irma," I said, and Mal and I walked her to the door. I closed and locked it and returned to the couch. Mal jumped up and curled up beside me. I spent the next hour going through the yearbooks and writing down the names of the boys Frances went to school with. Then I noticed Manfred Engle. He didn't run in the same circles as Frances, but he was always with another boy. That boy was Thomas Olway—Betty's husband.

I thumbed through the books and noticed that Thomas was in a lot of the same activities as Frances, only he was always pictured on the other side of the group from her. That's when I noticed a picture from Frances's sophomore year. She was in a play, *The Importance of Being Earnest*, and so was Thomas Olway.

Maybe there was a connection there. I put the books up and got ready for bed. In the morning, I'd go see Frances. Maybe she would tell me who Kayla's grandfather was. Maybe it was Thomas Olway. Maybe that was the connection to Manfred, not Frances. If I could prove it, it would take Frances off the suspect list.

There was just one problem. Men didn't usually murder by poison. But no matter. Who's to say he didn't do it on purpose to throw off the police? Time would tell.

Chapter 13

Sunday morning, with no fudge to make, I made a casserole for Frances. I stopped by after church service and knocked on the door. Mal was with me as we peered into the front window surrounded by Christmas lights.

"Oh, Allie, come in," Douglas said as he opened the door. "The sun is out but it's still cold enough to freeze your nose off."

We walked in and I wiped my feet on the rug as he closed the door. "How's Frances doing? I brought you a casserole."

"Thanks, but you didn't have to do that. Frances is doing better," he said. "She spent yesterday with Sally."

"Douglas, who is it?" Frances came out from the kitchen. "Allie! Mal! Good to see you." She came over and gave me a quick hug and picked Mal up. The pup licked her cheek. "What's this?"

"A casserole," I said. "Based on a shepherd's pie recipe. I thought you might not want to cook."

"Douglas, can you put that in the fridge so Allie can take off her coat and stay awhile?"

He took the dish from my hands and left the room. I hung up my coat and slipped out of my snow boots, leaving them to dry in the boot tray near the door. The living room looked just as sparkly in the daytime as it had at night. There was a fire in the fireplace. A Christmas tree filled the far corner, offering sparkling ornaments and ribbons. It had a plaid tree skirt. The fireplace mantel was draped with pine boughs, pinecones, and white twinkle lights.

"Your home looks wonderful," I said. "I can't believe you are unpacking and still decorated for the season."

Frances smiled slightly. "I love Christmas."

I sat down on the couch. "How are you?"

"Better," she said. "There's something freeing about having your deepest secrets discovered."

"I heard you spent the day with Sally," I said. "Does she still think you killed Kayla?"

"No," Frances said. "I think she's come to realize I had nothing to do with it. Of course, Manfred's death helped a bit. I hated to hear about it."

"They suspect Manfred and Kayla were poisoned by fudge and Rex is sending in inspectors." I leaned back. "They are supposed to come tomorrow to inspect the apartment kitchen, the McMurphy, and possibly your kitchen, since I made fudge in all three places."

"Let them come," Frances said, and sat. Mal cuddled in her lap. "They won't find anything here."

"I told him that, but you know Rex . . ."

"He has to go through the steps and cover the bases, no matter how improbable," she said.

Douglas, bearing a tray of cookies and hot cocoa, came into the room. "They need to get this cleared up quickly to stop any bad press about Mackinac Island fudge. It's the height of the holiday selling season."

"That's what I told him," I said. "I spent two hours last night scheduling how I'm going to get all the fudge made and shipped once they approve of my kitchen."

"We'll help with the packing and shipping," Frances said.

"I don't know if you'll have time," I said. "The final inspections for the McMurphy are tomorrow. We have guests scheduled to return on Wednesday and we'll need to ensure everything goes well. The Santa Fun Run is coming up and it would be nice to have a full hotel."

"I know things have been crazy this year. Are you worried about the business?" Frances asked. "As your general manager, I want you to know that it's going to be all right. The insurance covered all the repairs and will keep us afloat until the summer season."

"I know, but I don't want our reputation soured by the roof collapse," I said. "I think the sooner we can prove we have safe, beautiful rooms for people to come back to, the better."

"They will come back," Douglas said as he took the

chair across from the couch and set the tray on the ottoman. "It's tradition."

"Speaking of tradition, the ladies came to see me last night," I said as I picked up my cup of hot cocoa.

"What ladies?" Douglas asked.

"Frances's book club," I said, and sipped my cocoa.

Frances picked up a mug of cocoa and settled back in the chair without disturbing Mal in her lap. "They didn't bother you, did they?"

"No," I said, "but it would have been nice to know they might show up. Mostly they were worried about you, Frances."

"I'll be fine."

"Why didn't you two tell me that they had a poison guy come and speak to the senior center?"

"It didn't occur to me to mention it," Douglas said, and snagged a ginger cookie off the plate.

"Mrs. Tunisian told me about it and said that all the seniors know about aconite as a poison," I said.

"Aconite?" Frances asked.

"Yes, it's what the lab found in both Kayla and Manfred." I paused and leaned in closer. "Can I ask a very personal question?"

Frances stiffened. "That depends . . ."

My heart pounded in my chest. If I insulted Frances I could lose her and Douglas and they were the only friends I had left to help me run the hotel. But I felt she held the clue as to who was doing this. "Can you tell me who Sally's father was? Before you get upset, I'm not asking to be nosy. I think he might be the key to the case."

"Men don't generally poison," Douglas said.

Frances stayed quiet. The sound of her lack of answer was deafening. "It's okay," I rushed. "Don't answer that. I just worry that you're still the only link between Kayla and Manfred. I want to find this killer so we can go on with our lives."

Frances was very still. Then she sighed and sipped her cocoa. Mal looked up at her after the sigh as if to ask what was wrong. "Unfortunately, my life will never be the same and neither will Sally's. Even after they find this killer, everything is different now. I noticed it in church this morning. People look at me differently."

"For something that happened over fifty years ago when you were sixteen?" I shook my head. "Everyone does stupid stuff when they are teenagers. It's part of being human."

"It's also not paraded through town," Frances said. "At least I'm no longer teaching."

"It's the killer who should be shamed," I said strongly. "Not you. From what I can tell, Sally lived a good life and so did Kayla."

"Sally did say her parents treated her well. The only reason Kayla came looking for me is because she took a DNA test and discovered that her grandparents weren't her biological grandparents."

"Does Sally know who her father is?" I asked.

"It didn't come up," Frances said, drawing her eyebrows together in consternation. "I took the DNA test because I was researching my heritage. I had no idea this would happen."

"I have been reading a few articles on DNA tests. It seems there are some real stories of lost family members, et cetera," Douglas said.

"I never told Sally's father," Frances said quietly.

"You never told him?" I asked. "Why?"

"He had a fiancée and family obligations," she said. "I never told him." She put down her cup. "It was fifty-four years ago. He was five years older than me and I wasn't going to ruin both our lives."

Well, that ruled out my Thomas Olway theory. Thomas was only a year older than Frances. "But surely you could tell him now," I said.

"He's dead," she said, and looked at Douglas. "I looked him up on Sally's birthday every year. He died about eighteen months ago in a car accident. Silly, but I thought that meant the whole thing was over."

"So what's the connection to Manfred? Did he know about Sally?" I asked. "He lived above you all those years."

"No, I don't think so," Frances said. "I don't think anyone knew about Sally's father and me. I didn't even tell my mother who the boy was."

"Why not?" I asked.

"She didn't want to talk about it," Frances said, strangely calm. "She sent me off to Saginaw and that was that. I kept pretty much to myself for a long time until I met my Richard. When he died, I thought that was it for me until Douglas came along." She smiled at him. "I've been a lucky woman." Her gaze came back to mine. "I don't think Sally's father's family would want to be involved."

"But doesn't Sally want to know? If for no other reason than to understand her family health history?"

"Actually, no, she's not interested," Frances said. "She told me she had asked Kayla not to look into it because she doesn't want to know. She wants to preserve her memories of the parents who raised her and I respect that decision."

"You're right," I said, backing down. "The father probably doesn't have anything to do with this. Frances, do you know anyone who would want to hurt Manfred or frame you?"

"I've been over this and over this," Frances said, and grew fidgety. "I don't know anyone who would want to frame me or hurt Manfred. People loved him. He was always the life of the party in person."

"Yes, but with computers and social media, you don't have to meet people face-to-face to make enemies these days. All you have to do is state an unpopular opinion and people are all over you." I drank the last of my hot cocoa. "Did Manfred have a computer?"

"I don't know," Frances said. "I tend to keep my computer work at work, if you know what I mean. When I get home, that's time for friends and family and face-to-face. I hate seeing everyone staring at their phones instead of talking to each other."

"Hear! Hear!" Douglas said. "I don't think people know how to interact with each other in person anymore."

"Both Kayla and Manfred were poisoned—that seems pretty intimate. I hardly think a killer would trust sending candy through the mail."

"True," Douglas said. "The killer would want to hand-deliver it to ensure the right person was poisoned."

"As long as it wasn't random poisoning," Frances said.

"They found boxes of my and a couple other fudge makers's fudge in Manfred's and Kayla's apartments."

"That means you or one of us sold candy to the killer," Frances said.

"Unless they bought it online," I mused, feeling slightly horrified that I might indeed have interacted with the killer.

"Let's change the subject," Frances said after a long pause. "I understand you don't have a Christmas tree yet."

"I was hoping to set one up in the McMurphy," I said.

"We could go and find one for the apartment and the McMurphy," Frances said. "You can never have too many Christmas trees."

"We can get some artificial ones," Douglas pointed out. "They don't leave needles."

"I prefer real trees," I said. "They are sustainable. Think about the fact that they live and grow for years, giving us oxygen and providing cover for birds. Then we cut them down and they bring us a lovely smell and are so pretty and natural. When we are done, I always ensure they go to the chipper to be made into mulch to nourish the gardens. Now, what has your artificial tree done for the environment?"

"I didn't realize you were such an environmentalist," Douglas said, and sipped his drink. "My artificial tree is easy to put up and take down and it doesn't leave a mess. Plus, it's prestrung with lights so there's no mess of lights to straighten out. It's efficient and if I put some tree-scented ornaments on it, it has all the look and scent of a real tree."

I glanced at Frances. She shrugged then winked. "We'll get us a couple of real trees. You should put one up in the apartment in the McMurphy, too."

"I will after it passes inspection. No sense in decorating if there's more work to be done."

"You should take two sleds when you go," Douglas said. "To help you haul a tree each—that is, if you plan on buying more than one."

"Pete Thompson will deliver a tree for an additional twenty-five dollars," Frances said. "His crew will deliver it, cut a chunk off the bottom, and set it up in a tree stand and double-check that it won't fall, all before leaving."

"Sounds like that might be worth twenty-five dollars," I said. "Have you ever tried to cut the end off of a Christmas tree? It's harder than you think—even with a thin saw."

"Sounds like you've had practice," Douglas said.

"I have," I said. "When do you want to go?"

"Let's go now," Frances said. "While the sun is out."

"Great," I said. "Come on, Mal, let's go get ourselves a couple of Christmas trees."

Twenty minutes later Mal, Frances, and I were on our way to the Christmas tree lot run by St. Anne's

Church. I pulled a wooden sled with metal skids and held Mal's leash as she walked ahead of us, eager to be on the way to somewhere. Frances also pulled a sled. I had decided to skip the tree delivery and enjoy putting up the tree myself. The air was crisp and smelled of snow—Christmas smells to me. My parents used to let me visit Grammy Alice and Papa Liam over Christmas break. It was late afternoon and the sun was already setting, causing the Christmas lights surrounding the lot to glow bright.

"All right, Mal," I said. "Our goal is to find two perfect Christmas trees."

"What do you define as perfect?" Frances asked.

"Well, they are both for apartments, so no more than six foot tall," I said. "I like a fir tree with small soft needles that are firm enough to hold ornaments without drooping and the tree should be full and round."

"You haven't thought about this much, have you?" Frances laughed.

"Sarcasm will get you nowhere," I teased. "Those are my goals, but that said, I do love the imperfections of a real tree. Last year's tree had a crooked trunk, but I was able to get it in the tree stand at an angle that gave the illusion it was a straight tree."

"So you have big dreams of the perfect tree, but then you purchase the Charlie Brown tree," she said—meaning the *Peanuts* character.

I shrugged. "I have a soft heart."

"That's no surprise," Frances said. I was glad to see her perked up. The last few days had been so hard on her. I was afraid she would never recover. But then, who wouldn't be happy on their way to pick up a Christmas tree?

The lot was not large, perhaps fourteen feet by fourteen feet. There were a handful of trees standing in the center and a row of trees leaning against the fence that surrounded the lot. At least four families were inside looking for the perfect tree. A man stood inside the lot, holding trees up for a woman to inspect as she walked the perimeter.

"Hey, Frances, Allie," Paul Binder greeted us as we left the sleds outside the fence and stepped into the lot. He was a kind man with smiling blue eyes. I had met him once or twice at a chamber of commerce kaffeeklatsch. He wore a knit cap, a flannel shirt with a puffy vest, gloves, jeans, and thick boots. His cheeks were rosy from the cold. "I see two sleds. Does that mean you're both looking for trees?"

"Actually, I'm looking for two trees," I said. "I've been informed that I should have a tree in both apartments."

"You have two apartments?" His eyes twinkled. "Must be nice to be so rich."

"I'm not rich," I protested. "I'm staying in Frances's place right now but the McMurphy should be habitable after tomorrow's inspections."

"I'm teasing," he said, letting me off the hook. "You can have trees in every room of the McMurphy if you want. I'd be happy to deliver them. I work part time for Pete."

"I don't think I need that many," I said. "Thanks, though."

"You ladies take your time and let me know when

you find the perfect tree." He walked off to greet the next family coming into the lot.

We walked the perimeter. I loved the crunch of the packed snow under my feet and the scent of cut pine.

"Here's a nice one," Frances said, and lifted up a tree that was about five feet tall.

"Oh, I do like that," I said as she twirled it to view it from all angles. It was a fir tree and had only a few gaps in the branches. "How's the trunk?"

"Looks fairly straight," Frances said, assessing it.

"Great," I said, and took the tree from her. "I'll put this on a sled while you keep looking." I gave her Mal's leash and picked up the tree. "Hey, Paul, I found one."

"Let me net it for you," he said, and took the tree from me. In the back of the lot was a machine. He put the tree into the mouth of the machine, put his foot on a pedal, and the tree shot through the machine, coming out the other end bagged in netting. "Pretty neat trick, huh?"

"Yes," I said as I took the tree from him. "It's certainly easier to transport netted."

"I rented it from Mackinaw City."

"Smart," I said. "Can I pay when we find the second tree?"

"Sure," he said. "I know where you live."

That was the wonderful thing about small towns. There was a level of trust between residents because we truly did know where one another lived. I sobered a moment. It also meant that a local killer knew where everyone lived as well. Shaking off the thought, I carried the tree to the sled and tied it on. It was Christmastime and picking out the tree was supposed to be fun. I couldn't let morbid thoughts overtake me.

I walked back to Frances to find her talking to a family. There was a man and woman and a small girl who petted Mal.

"I asked if I could pet your dog," the little girl said. "She's so cute!"

"It's always a good thing to ask before you pet a dog," I said, and squatted down to get on her level. "Her name is Mal. She loves to get petted."

"She's soft," the little girl said. Her hand was bare, her mitten dangling from her wrist, where it was attached to a string. I remembered that kind of mitten, the knitted kind with a long string that went from one wrist to the other. My mom would slide the string around the back of my neck and put my coat on over it so that no matter how hard I played I wouldn't lose my mittens.

"Come on, Stacy," the mom said. "We're here to pick out our Christmas tree."

The little girl's eyes lit up as she straightened. "Santa is coming in a few weeks. We have to get the perfect tree."

"I'm sure you'll find it," I said, and stood. Frances and I watched as the little girl ran from tree to tree, chattering to her parents about what she liked or didn't like. "Christmas is even more special when you have children."

"Yes, it is," Frances said. She sounded melancholy.

"Are you okay?"

"I was just thinking of all the Christmases I missed with Sally." Her eyes glistened in the light, but she was smiling. "I always thought I would have more children, but it wasn't meant to be. I guess that's why I loved teaching. Every year I had new children in my life and I got to watch them grow up and have families of their own."

I gave her a quick hug. "I'm so sorry that I never knew what you sacrificed."

"I didn't want anyone to know," she whispered. "It was shameful."

"Babies are never shameful," I said. "Now, let's find the perfect tree for my new apartment in the McMurphy." I distracted her with silly comments on the pluses and minuses of each tree.

We decided on the second tree, Paul netted it for us, and I paid as Frances tied it to her sled. Mal pulled me out of the lot, toward Frances.

"Let's get some hot cocoa," I said. "I think the Lucky Bean is open."

"But it's in the opposite direction," Frances pointed out.

"So, a little walk won't hurt us," I said. "Are you up for it?"

"Sure—why not?" Frances said. We picked up our sled ropes and happily pulled our trees toward the marina. We were halfway there when Frances's phone rang. She stopped and pulled it out.

"Is it Douglas?" I asked. "Should we buy him some hot cocoa?"

"It's not Douglas," she said, and frowned. "It's a number I don't recognize."

"Maybe just a robocall," I said. "Let it go to voice mail. If it's important, they'll leave a message."

"I hate to do that," she said.

"Seriously, it's what I do. If it's important they'll leave a message and you can call them right back."

The phone went silent in her hand. "I guess that's smart," she said with a shrug. "Come on, let's get cocoa. I'm sure whoever it was wouldn't mind if I called back in a few minutes."

We parked our sleds outside and Frances and Mal and I walked into the heat of the coffee shop on the marina. It was a small shop with a few café chairs and tables. "Hi, Angie," I said as we entered. "We'd like two—"—I paused and looked at Frances—"Should we get one for Douglas?"

"Yes, let's."

"Okay." I turned back to Angie at the counter. "Let's get three large hot cocoas with whipped cream to go, please."

"I'm on it," Angie said. "We've had a lot of people in for cocoa today. 'Tis the season."

I turned to see Frances listening on her phone and turning very white. "Frances?" I grabbed her as she crumpled. "What is it?"

She handed me her phone. I hit REPLAY on the message.

"Frances . . ." came a whisper. "Do you know where your daughter is?"

"What is this?" I asked as I guided her to a chair.

"I don't know," she said with a shake of her head. "But I have a terrible feeling."

"I'll call Douglas."

"No," she said. "Call Rex. Have him check on Sally."

"Didn't she go back to Saginaw?" I asked.

"No," Frances said. "She is staying on the island until they find her daughter's killer." She looked at me with fear in her large brown eyes. "What if the killer got to Sally, too?"

RED VELVET FUDGE

1½ cups white chocolate chips
2 ⅓ cups sweetened condensed milk
Green food coloring
24 ounces milk chocolate chips
¼ cup unsweetened cocoa powder
Red food coloring

Prepare an 8 x 8-inch square pan by lining with foil and buttering foil. Melt white chocolate chips and ⅓ cup sweetened condensed milk in a small saucepan. Stir continuously, careful not to burn the chocolate. Remove from heat and divide into two. Add green food coloring to one and stir. Leave the second mixture white.

In a medium microwave-safe bowl, combine milk chocolate chips, 2 cups sweetened condensed milk, and cocoa powder. Microwave on high for 1 minute. Stir. Continue to microwave and stir in 30-second intervals until chips are melted and mixture is smooth. Add red food coloring. Pour into prepared pan. Drizzle green and white fudge over the top. Swirl with a cold butter knife.

Chill until set. Cut into 1-inch-square pieces. Enjoy!

Makes 64 pieces of fudge.

Chapter 14

"Take Frances home," Rex said on the other end of the phone. "I'll go check on Sally."

"She's staying at the Filmores' cottage," I said, and looked at Frances for acknowledgment. She nodded. "Call us as soon as you know she's all right."

"I will." He hung up the phone.

"Cocoas are ready," Angie said from the counter, and held out a tray of cups.

"Thanks," I said, paid for the cocoa, and grabbed the tray. "Come on, Frances, let's get you back to Douglas until Rex can figure out what's going on."

"Right." Frances had Mal in her lap. She stood and put the pup down. "Let's get to Douglas. Do you think that was the killer who called? Do you think he poisoned Sally? Who would hurt people during Christmas?"

I put my arm through hers, and Mal picked up her leash and followed us out. We grabbed our sleds and took off at a brisk pace toward Frances's house. "We can only wait and see," I said. "I'll feel better once we're with Douglas."

Frances glanced at me. "Do you think we're in danger?"

"No," I said with more certainty than I felt. "This killer uses poison. They are a coward. Besides, Mal will protect us."

Mal barked with her leash in her mouth and ran ahead of us on the plowed sidewalk. We hurried back to Frances's home and Douglas opened the door as we left the trees in the yard and hurried up the porch.

"Are you okay?" Douglas asked.

"Yes," Frances said as we stomped the snow from our boots and unbuttoned our coats.

"Did Rex call you and tell you what was going on?" I asked.

"Yes," Douglas said, and hugged Frances. "He said for me to take your phone. They may need it to trace the call."

"The caller left a message," I said. "That's pretty bold." I pulled off my boots and made my way in stockinged feet to the living room couch. I put the tray of cocoas on the coffee table. "We got you a hot chocolate."

He guided Frances to the chair in front of the fire. I pulled out a cup and handed it to her. "Rex should call fairly soon and let us know what's going on," Douglas said.

"I'm worried about Sally," Frances said as she wrapped her hands around her paper cup of not-so-hot chocolate.

"The caller left a message," I repeated. "That

means they aren't afraid of us finding out that they are a man."

"The whisper was creepy," Frances said. "What if it was intentional to mask their voice? I mean, they have devices that do that, right? Change your voice? What if they were using one and that is why they left a message? They know we will never be able to match their voice."

"We can't jump to any conclusions," Douglas said, and took her hand in his. "It could just be a prank call."

"Do you have Sally's phone number?" I asked. "You can call her."

"I don't," Frances said. "If I did have it, I would have called her before I called Rex."

"Of course," I said. "Funny, she didn't give you her phone number."

Frances sent me a quick smile, then looked down at her cup. "She didn't want to be connected like that." She looked at me. "She said she saw no reason for us to keep in touch and I suppose she's right."

"But the killer must think you keep in touch," I said. "Why else call you?"

"Indeed," Frances said.

"I'm worried," Douglas announced.

"Why?" Frances and I asked at the same time. It wasn't like Douglas to be worried or, worse, to admit it.

"This killer seems to be circling you," he said, and stood. "You could be next. I don't like it."

"I don't think they will hurt Frances," I said as I

watched Douglas go to the window and peer out. "They are framing her for the murders."

"We think they're framing her," he said as he stared outside. "But she may be the intended victim all along." He turned to us. "I don't want you out of my sight."

I looked at Frances. "He could be right. Don't eat or drink anything you haven't fixed yourself."

"That goes the same for you two," Frances said, her lips thin and tight. "If they want to hurt me, then they will target you." We put the untouched hot cocoas back in the tray.

My phone rang and we all jumped. "Nothing like being skittish," I muttered, and answered it on the second ring. "Hello?"

"Allie, are you with Frances?" It was Rex.

"Yes," I said. "We're at her house, like you said, and Douglas is here, too."

"Stay there, I'll be by shortly to talk."

"What's going on?" I asked.

"Sally seems to be missing," he said. "Just stay there."

"Okay," I said as he hung up.

"What is it?" Frances asked.

"Rex is coming over. He said that Sally seems to be missing."

"Seems to be missing?" Frances sat at the edge of her seat. "Is he sure?"

"She could have just gone back home," Douglas said.

"I'm sure the police are checking into that," I said.

"Frances, if you don't have Sally's phone number, did she have yours?"

"Why?" Douglas asked.

"How else would the caller know to call Frances and leave that awful message?" I said, then leaned toward her. "You gave Sally your number, didn't you?"

"Yes," Frances said.

"But you don't know Sally's number. So the killer could have called you from Sally's phone," I deduced.

"Maybe," Frances said, looking more pale with each passing moment.

"Most likely we know the killer," Douglas said. "Which means they already knew your number."

"Why are they doing this?" Frances asked, and rubbed her hands over her face. "It's Christmas, for goodness' sake."

There was a knock on the door and Douglas answered it. I stood along with Frances as Rex stepped inside with a blast of icy air. He took off his hat and stomped the snow from his boots. "Thanks for letting me come by at dinnertime."

I glanced at my watch and saw it was six p.m. already. "I don't think we realized what time it was."

Rex nodded. "Frances, may I listen to the voice message?"

"Yes, of course," she said, and took him her phone. "Can I get you something to drink?"

"No, thank you," he said as he put the phone to his ear to listen to the message.

"I should put Allie's casserole in the oven to warm," Frances said, and stepped out of the living room.

"Talk to me about Sally," Douglas said. "Allie said you told her Sally was missing. Are you certain she didn't simply leave the island to go back home to her husband?"

"No one saw her leave," Rex said. "Officer Brown checked with the airport and no planes have landed or taken off. The ferry's last run was at three p.m. Sally wasn't on it." He glanced at me. "When was the last time you saw Sally?"

"Me? A few days ago when she came to visit Frances," I said. "I never really got to talk to her."

"Douglas?" Rex asked.

"She was here yesterday for an hour," he said. "Frances was trying to comfort her. I'm not sure it took."

"You think she wasn't in a good state of mind?" Rex asked.

"Would you be if your only child was murdered?" Douglas replied.

"No, I guess not," Rex said.

"Do you think she hurt herself?" I asked. "If so, why would someone call and leave that message?"

"I'm just looking at all the possibilities," Rex said. "Do you know if Sally was familiar with the island?"

"This was the first time she had visited," Frances said as she came out of the kitchen. "Please, come sit down." She waved toward the couch. We all sat. Rex had removed his boots and sat on the front edge of the wing-backed chair. He seemed alert yet relaxed. "Sally told me that she had avoided the island her whole life because she knew I lived here and she didn't want to run into me, even accidentally."

I winced at the pain in Frances's voice.

Frances studied Rex. "You believe she is missing?"

"When we got to where she's staying, we knocked but there was no answer. I contacted the rental property owner. He gave me Sally's number and the number she left for her husband. Sally didn't answer her phone and her husband said as far as he knew, Sally had not left the island."

"So the killer kidnapped her?" Douglas asked.

"We can't be certain," Rex said. "I've got patrolmen out looking for her. She could have simply gone for a walk."

"In the dark, by herself?" I pointed out.

"It's Christmas," Rex said. "Lots of people go out to see the lighting displays."

"But no one has seen her," Frances stated.

"No, not that we know of," Rex said. "I came here to listen to the message myself. It could be a prank call."

"What a horrible prank," Frances said, and touched her throat. "If it is the killer, why take Sally? I mean, he poisoned Kayla. Why not simply try to poison Sally?"

"The word is out on the poison," Rex said. "He may have felt the need to take matters in his . . . or her . . . own hands."

"I just don't know why this is happening," Frances said, and covered her face with her hands.

"Frances," Rex said. "Who is Sally's father?"

"Why is that important?" Frances said. "I haven't seen him in decades and he died over a year ago."

"Just tell me," Rex said. "It might be important."

Frances blew out a long breath and sat back. "Fine, I guess it doesn't matter. His name is John Ellsworth. His family has a cottage on the island, but he rarely stayed here. I think he lived in Chicago."

Rex wrote down the name. "When was the last time you saw him?"

"Ten years ago," Frances said. "We had coffee."

"You said he died. Does his family still have property on the island?"

"I don't know," Frances said. "I suppose so. It was never that important to me."

"What did you talk about?"

"When?"

"When you saw him ten years ago. What did you talk about?" Rex asked.

"This and that at first," Frances said. "You see, I never told him about the baby. I didn't want him to think I wanted anything from him or his family. But his wife had died and I thought he should know . . . you know, in case he wanted to meet her."

"What did he say?"

"He was shocked at first, then wanted to know everything. I told him that I only knew she was a girl and that the adoption was closed. He asked where I had her and I told him. That was the last time I saw him."

"Do you know if Sally contacted him?" Rex asked.

"I doubt it," Frances said. "She didn't want to contact me."

"Do you know if he contacted Sally?" Rex pushed.

"If he did, she didn't say," Frances said. "Allie

thought the killer might have something to do with Sally's father, but I don't see why. As far as I know he only came back to the island that one time. It's a small place. I would have known if he vacationed here for any length of time."

"I know these are painful memories," Rex said. "But any information you have can help. Is there anything else that you know?"

"No," Frances said, still holding her throat. "It was a closed adoption. Sally didn't even want Kayla to find me. I respected her decision. John was a summer mistake when I was sixteen. I had hoped to never talk about it. But I guess we all have to face our mistakes."

I hugged Frances. "You were sixteen and thought you were in love."

"Did you know Sally Cramdon was your daughter?" Rex asked gently.

"Not until you told me about Kayla," Frances said. "Now Kayla's dead and Sally is missing. Is Sally's husband coming?"

"I've asked him to stay home in case Sally shows up there," Rex said.

"It's probably safer," Douglas said. "It seems someone on the island is after his family."

"Did you look into Sally's ex-husband?" I asked. "Does his family own property? Is he a regular visitor to the island? Could this be about him and not Frances?"

"Phillip Cramdon is a manufacturing manager in Saginaw," Rex said. "His family doesn't own property here. He has an alibi, and we were able to rule him out of Kayla's murder. He told us no threats were ever made against him."

"Why isn't he on the island with Sally, looking into his daughter's death?" I asked.

"He couldn't get time off," Rex said.

"But his daughter is dead," I stated the obvious.

"Apparently he only gets one week's leave. He came the first day, settled Sally in, and answered questions. When I told him the investigation would be ongoing he left. He told Sally he wanted to be able to go to his daughter's funeral and to do that he couldn't waste time off while we investigate."

"Seems heartless," I said.

"If he's in manufacturing, they may not have the money to take unpaid leave," Douglas said. "It's not heartless if it's what he has to do to pay the bills."

"Right."

"Rex, were you able to get into her rental place?" Frances asked. "She could be passed out on the floor or something."

"The landlord let us in," Rex said. "Sally's suitcase and clothes were still there, but she wasn't." He stood. "I need to get back to the investigation. Call me if you get another message."

"I will," Frances said, and we all stood. Douglas walked Rex to the door and spoke to him quietly while he put on his boots and hat.

"I'm sorry this is all being dug up," I said, and hugged her. "It has to be hard to learn you have a granddaughter and lose her all within a few days and now your daughter is missing."

Frances seemed strangely calm. "I don't think I'm really comprehending what is happening." She hugged her waist. "Do you want to stay for dinner?"

At the word *dinner*, Mal perked up from where she slept near the fireplace. She rushed over to me and jumped up on my leg, her stubby tail wagging. "No," I said. "I should get the Christmas tree home and feed Mal and Mella."

"What about the second tree?" Frances said.

"We can keep it on the porch until tomorrow and take it to the McMurphy for you," Douglas said. "It should be fine outside for another day."

"Sounds perfect, thanks." I put on my coat, hat, and boots and tucked Mal into her winter coat and harness and leash. "Please keep me posted if you find out anything."

"We will," Douglas said. "Good night and thank you for the casserole."

"Good night," I said. Mal and I stepped out into the cold, clear night. In the distance I heard Christmas music playing. I grabbed the rope of my sled, leaving the second sled parked near Frances's porch, and Mal and I took off toward my rental.

Where was Sally Cramdon? Why would someone kidnap her? Was Frances the real target? If so, I hoped that Douglas could keep her safe.

I managed to get the tree upright in the tree stand and secure. It was a lot of work and I was pretty proud of myself. Of course, I had fed my pets first. I knew from watching my parents with their Christmas trees that setting up a real tree was usually a two-person job. It was also the time when my parents fought the most over how things should be done. Come to think of it, not having to set up a real tree anymore might be what saved their marriage.

"Well, Mal and Mella, I have to call this tree a success," I said as I lifted my mug of tea toward the bare tree in the front corner of the apartment. "It looks good here with the bookshelves and books, and when I get the lights on, people will be able to see it from the street. That's why you put your tree in front of the front window, you know."

I heard the foyer door slam and then someone pounded on my door. "Coming!"

A quick peek through the peephole told me it was Irma at the door. I opened it and she rushed in, still wearing her parka. "I heard that Sally Cramdon is missing. What can the girls and I do to help?"

"How did you—"

"Oh, come on, dear, the police have been out looking for her. What's the scoop? I know you know."

There was another knock on my door—this time it was Liz. I opened the door and she stormed in, wearing a parka with the fur-trimmed hood down, jeans, and knee-high boots with square heels and laces down the front. Her hair curled riotously around her head even though most of it was pulled back. "I heard about Sally," she said breathlessly. "What do you know?"

"Come in," I said as Mal bounced from one visitor

to the other. "Take your boots and coats off. I'll get us some tea." I glanced at Irma. "Are there more ladies coming?"

"I don't think so," she said. "It's Sunday night and there's a Christmas movie special on television."

"Right," I said, and went into the kitchen. I piled the tray with cups and tea bags, milk, and sugar and brought it into the living room to see that Barbara had shown up. "Hi, Barb, welcome. Find a seat, I'm bringing out the teakettle."

By the time the teakettle was hot, I heard my door open and close twice more. Mal was barking and running around. I brought the kettle out to see that Mary O'Malley and Mrs. Tunisian had arrived. I handed the teapot to Irma and grabbed Mal and tucked her safely into the cool bedroom with a fresh dog treat and a warm cuddle bed and closed the door behind her.

I turned to find Liz holding court from the arm of my couch.

"I heard that Frances got a voice message asking her if she knew where her daughter was and that's what started the investigation into Sally. Is that true, Allie?" Liz eyed me hopefully. "You were with her, right?"

"I can't confirm or deny for the record," I said, and picked up a mug and a bag of ginger apple spice tea. I unwrapped the bag and put it in my cup and poured hot water over it to steep. "Did anyone see Sally today? Rex said that her things were still in her rented cottage and no one had seen her leaving the island."

"I didn't see her," Liz said. "I've been leaving messages asking for an interview all week. I took a walk tonight to swing by her place and that's when I ran into Charles Brown. He told me she was missing and that a mysterious message on Frances's phone started them looking."

"I saw her yesterday," Irma said. "She was talking to Patrick Damon on Market Street."

"Why would she be talking to him?" I wondered out loud. "Do they know each other?"

"I thought he helped you do CPR on Kayla," Mrs. Tunisian said. "Maybe she was asking him about that."

"Oh, that's true," I said. "I wasn't thinking about that."

"Speaking of Patrick, I heard that his uncle died and he hopes to inherit the old man's fortune," Mary O'Malley said. "My son Bobby said Patrick was bragging about it at the bar last week. Seems his uncle's wife died ten years ago and they had no children. Patrick told Bobby he was set for life."

"What does that have to do with Sally?" I asked.

"Oh, it doesn't," Mary said. "I thought we were talking about Patrick, such a strange boy. Did you know that now he wants to live on the island year-round. Wait, you don't think he took Sally, do you?"

"Why would he do that?" I asked.

"Well, because you were talking about him," Mary said, and shrugged. "I thought maybe you suspected him."

"Patrick tried to save Kayla," Liz said. "He has no reason to kill her or take Sally."

"Besides, everyone knows that poison means the killer is a woman," Barbara said with a firm nod.

"But women don't generally kidnap other women," Betty said. "Do they?"

"Statistically women are more likely to kidnap kids," Liz said. "Usually to gain custody of their child."

"But Sally is a grown woman," Irma pointed out. "It's hard to kidnap a grown woman."

"It is," I said. I had been kidnapped once and I knew it was no walk in the park. "So why would a man kidnap Sally, if a woman killed Kayla and Manfred?"

"Also, how is all this related to Manfred Engle?" Liz asked. "I have done some digging and for the life of me I can't find a connection."

"Well, we can't just sit around here and do nothing," Irma said. "I'm going to tell Rex we want to send out search parties. I'm sure we can each gather enough people to walk through the parks looking for her. She might be out there, lost, and freezing. She could die of exposure."

"Calling Rex is a good idea," I said. "You do that. Liz, can you help me in the kitchen a minute?"

"Sure." Liz stood and followed me into the tiny back kitchen, where I put fresh water in the teapot and put it on its heating element to boil. "What do you know?"

"It's not what I know," I said, keeping my voice low. "It's what you can find out. You have access to public records, right?"

"I have my sources," she said without blinking.

"I suppose I can wait until the town hall opens tomorrow and look through the records, but it might be too late by then."

"Too late for what?" she asked, her voice matching mine in tone.

"For Sally," I said. "Look, I don't know if there's a connection, but Frances told us that Sally's father was John Ellsworth. Apparently he spent a few summers on the island in the 1960s. I don't know if it's related, but . . ."

"It's something to look into," Liz said.

"What's something to look into?" Carol asked as she came into the crowded kitchen.

"Buying an artificial tree," I said. "I was telling her how hard it was to haul and set up my real tree."

"You have a tree?" Carol said. "Where?"

"In the den, facing the open window," I said, and gave Liz a look. She nodded in response. "It took me over an hour to get it up. I need to let it rest overnight before I add lights and ornaments."

"I think real trees are better no matter how difficult," Carol said, and put her hands on her hips.

"The artificial-versus-real-tree debate is a great article for this week's paper," Liz said as she wrote in her notebook.

"We aren't here to talk about trees," Carol said. "Allie, do you have any fudge?"

"I always have fudge," I said. "There's some in the freezer. It might take an hour or two to thaw."

"Any cookies?" Carol asked. "The ladies find solving murders gives them the munchies."

"Is that what we're doing?" I asked. "Solving murders?"

"Of course," Carol said. "We're here to save Frances's daughter, Sally. If you don't have cookies or fudge, crackers and cheese will do."

"I'll see what I can dig up," I said, and handed the hot teapot to Liz. The two ladies left the kitchen as I gathered up a tray full of saltines and slices of Swiss cheese. I arranged them haphazardly on a plate and hurried out to the living room. "Here's some snack food. So what is the plan to help Sally?"

"Well," Barbara said. "We are setting up a call tree to let everyone know Sally is missing and try to piece together her last known whereabouts. Do you have a whiteboard or a large sheet of paper?"

"Why?"

"So we can keep track of the time line," Irma said as she put cheese on a cracker and ate it.

"No, unfortunately, I don't," I said. "I do have a notebook."

"That will do in a pinch," Mary said.

I grabbed a notebook and pen and sat down. "Do you think we should let Rex know we're doing this? We don't want to step on the toes of the official investigation."

"Oh dear, no," Barbara said. "He would simply tell us to stop and then waste his precious time worrying about us. Trust me, we can get through the calls in an hour."

"We've already divided the list of residents," Carol said. "What you need to do is to write down the people who know something so we can construct a time line. It will be simple, really. Mackinac is a small island."

I settled in as the ladies started dialing. Perhaps it was better to keep an eye on the ladies than let them go somewhere else to cause mischief. That's what I would tell Rex, anyway, when he'd ask how everyone knew Sally was missing.

Chapter 15

"That's it," Irma said as she put down her cell phone. "The last person on the list and it's only ten p.m. Allie, what do we know?"

I looked over my notes. "It looks like Sally was last seen by Mrs. Thompson as she entered her rental at four p.m. with a bag of groceries from Doud's."

"Elaine reported that Sally was alone," Mary said. "So whoever kidnapped her must have been waiting for her in the rental."

"And they didn't go out the front of the rental as a couple of residents had eyes on the street and didn't see anything unusual," Irma said. "What time did Frances receive the phone call?"

"I think it was nearly five," I said. "We were picking out Christmas trees."

"Okay, so Sally went missing and within an hour Frances got the phone call," Liz said. "They didn't leave the island, and no one saw her after that." Liz tapped the end of her pen on her chin thoughtfully. "The rental backs up to the park. They must have gone out the back and into the park."

"The kidnapper has to be local," Barbara said. "Otherwise someone would have mentioned seeing a fudgie in the neighborhood, wouldn't they?"

"There are a couple of rentals in that neighborhood," Irma pointed out. "So it could be a renter."

"No, if any of those renters seemed suspicious, we would know," Mary argued.

"I'm sure the police have knocked on all the doors in that area," Carol said. "I think it's safe to assume that the kidnapper is a local who knows the area and took her out through the park. They could have gone down Arch Park Road and into any number of residences along there."

"It couldn't be far," Irma said. "Or someone would have seen something. The leaves are off the trees."

"But it was also dark and people are pretty focused on Christmas right now," I said. "Not so much looking for a couple walking by."

"Oh yes, he could have had his arm around her to control her and people might mistake that for a loving couple on a walk," Carol suggested.

"I think we should knock on doors within fifty yards of her rental," Barbara said.

"I think the police are already doing that," Liz pointed out. "I highly doubt they would want us doing the same thing." She stood. "Come on, ladies. It's getting late and I understand Allie has to meet with inspectors in the morning."

"Oh yes, I have to meet with the kitchen inspectors and the building inspectors," I said, and stood to help usher them out. "You all have my phone number. Text me if you think of anything."

Barbara yawned. "Good idea. Who knew sleuthing could be so exhausting?" She stood and helped Mary up. "Besides, now that the entire island knows Sally is missing it will be extremely difficult for the kidnapper to hide. I'm guessing Rex and his crew will find Sally by noon tomorrow."

"If not, we'll meet again here tomorrow," Irma said.

"Sounds like a good plan," Carol said. The ladies put on their coats and hats and boots.

"Does anyone need me to walk you home?" I asked. "It's late and the streets aren't exactly safe."

"Oh, we're fine," Carol said with a dismissive wave of her hand. "Anyone tries to get me and they will be in a world of hurt." She patted her coat pocket. "I have a Taser."

Mary nodded. "I have pepper spray. We'll be fine."

"Okay," I said. "Text me when you get home so that I know you are safe."

"We will," the ladies said.

"We are home," Irma quipped as she gestured between herself and Barbara. "Unless you want us to text you from the other side of the house."

"I'm sure you're fine," I said. "But if you ever find yourself in danger you can always call me."

Liz stayed with me while the ladies left. As soon as Irma closed her door, Liz pulled me aside. "I did some digging on my tablet."

"You brought your tablet?" I asked.

She glanced up at the foyer and then closed the door so that we were alone in my apartment. "I take notes on it and it has access to the Internet, so yes, I brought my tablet. I looked into John Ellsworth's connections on the island. Did you know he was Patrick Damon's uncle?"

"What? Really? So Patrick is Sally's cousin?"

"And according to the public record, John died eighteen months ago, leaving no children and no will."

"Patrick did say he was planning on inheriting the family home," I mused.

"There's more," she said. "I checked with a friend of mine who is involved in the probate court system. The estate is being contested. It seems when Kayla did her DNA test, she was put in touch with John's relatives."

"As his daughter, Sally would have been set to inherit his estate," I surmised.

"Kayla was the one to hire a lawyer to look into the possibility," Liz said.

"Then someone killed Kayla and now has kidnapped Sally," I said. "Do you think it's Patrick?"

"Men don't usually poison people. They are more straightforward killers."

"Then who? Does Patrick have a large family?"

"I heard his mother died last year and he only has a distant cousin on his father's side," Liz said.

"Is the Ellsworth property near the park?"

"Yes. See?" She showed me the address on her tablet.

"We need to call Rex. Patrick might have taken Sally."

"We can't involve the police without proof," Liz said. "Why don't you get your snow gear on? We can get over there and check it out. If we see anything suspicious then we can call Rex."

"All right," I said, and yanked on my coat, hat, and boots. "Let's take Mal. Then if we're questioned we can say we were taking the dog for a walk."

"Sounds like a plan," Liz said. "We can say you were walking me home and taking Mal for a walk."

"But the Ellsworth place is in the opposite direction of your home," I pointed out.

"Does that really matter?" Liz grinned at me.

I opened the bedroom door and my pup bounded out, wagging her little stub tail. "Come on, Mal, let's do some sleuthing." I put on her coat and halter and attached the leash and we went outside with Liz. I glanced over my shoulder as we stepped off the porch and waved at Irma, who was peering out her window. "We're being watched," I said, smiling with gritted teeth.

"Always," Liz said with a laugh. "Come on, let's walk toward my place and then backtrack toward the Ellsworth property."

"Do you really think Patrick has something to do with this? I mean, do guys use poison? Plus, he helped me try to save Kayla. Why would he do that if he wanted her dead?"

"I am not sure," Liz said. "If I was sure, I would have called Rex."

"It must have been exciting for Kayla to take the DNA test and see who she might be related to."

"It led her to Mackinac Island and Frances," Liz concurred. "But it may have gotten her killed." We walked in silence a moment. "Hey, did I see you sledding the other day with that new cute guy?"

"You mean Harry Wooston?" I asked.

"Is that his name? What did Rex say about it?"

"It was only a spontaneous sled ride and a cup of cocoa," I said. "It wasn't like it was a date. Besides, Rex has his hands full with Melonie."

"And it's nice to have some thoroughly male attention," Liz said. "Come on, let's take this road. It crosses behind the Ellsworth place."

"Who are you dating?" I probed.

"Well, I hear Trent Jessop is going to be back on the island next week to spend the holiday looking after the family businesses."

I stopped short. "You want to date Trent?"

"Mr. Tall, Dark, and Handsome?" Liz teased. "I had my shot at him years ago. He's gone too much to build a relationship."

"That's what I told him," I said.

"So we're both single . . . that is, if you're not serious about Harry."

"I'm not serious about anyone," I said. "I've got so much going on, what with the inspections and such."

"It seems that wouldn't keep a good man away," Liz said.

"Maybe he's just not that interested," I suggested.

"I'll ask around tomorrow and get you the skinny on him. I don't want you to get your heart broken."

I laughed. "My love life is full of heartbreak. There's nothing new about that." We arrived in the street behind the Ellsworth place. It was a large Victorian three-story with a garage and carriage house over the top.

"If she's in there, it will take a miracle to find her," I muttered. "The place is a mansion."

"It's just a cottage," Liz said. "For the rich and famous."

"Patrick doesn't live here," I said. He has a rental closer to the Grand Hotel."

"According to my notes, this is John Ellsworth's family home. Patrick was named the caretaker while the property is in probate. That means he has a key," she whispered. "Come on, let's look in the windows and see if anyone is here."

I glanced over my shoulder to see if anyone could see us as we walked up the drive toward the carriage house. Liz was correct the back of the property did butt up against the park. It was dark, but the snow reflected the moonlight. I looked for footprints, but there were none. Someone had shoveled a path around the carriage house to the park. Smart. In fact, there was a shoveled path around the entire home. I tapped Liz's shoulder as she peered into the back window.

"What?" she whispered.

"Isn't it weird that a house in probate has a path shoveled all around it? Even one beside the carriage house that goes straight to the path in the park." I used the flashlight app on my phone to point out the curious path. "That means anyone can come and go without leaving footprints."

"That is unusual," Liz said. "We can use it to our

advantage. I'll go around the back and see if I can see anything in the windows. You check out the carriage house. No one should be here. Let me know if you see anything."

"Okay." Mal and I headed toward the carriage house while Liz walked around the back of the house, looking in the windows. I glanced over at the neighboring house. Who lived there? Did they see who shoveled these paths? Did they know who comes and goes from the carriage house? I peered into the window of the door to the garage and shone my phone light. The garage was quiet and filled with the usual garage things: bikes, tools, shovels, and such. I looked into the second door's window. All I saw was a staircase up to the apartment above. There was a coat hanging on a hook by the door and boots neatly stacked underneath. It didn't look like anyone had been dragged up those stairs recently. I stepped back and looked up. The windows were dark and the entire property was ghostly quiet. I doubted Sally was in there.

Mal sniffed the path and we walked the perimeter. Maybe in the back there would be a light. Or on the off chance I was wrong and Sally was here, I might hear something suspicious. All I heard was the crunch of my footfalls on the shoveled walk. The back windows were dark. Suddenly Mal barked and I jumped with fright. "Shush," I said.

She barked again and pulled on her leash toward the main house. A light came on in a second-floor window. I swallowed and turned off my phone light to hide against the carriage house shadows. I picked up Mal and held her mouth closed to keep her from barking. I noticed the shadow of a man looking outside and I held my breath.

After what seemed an eternity, the man dropped the curtain and stepped back, and the light went out. I waited another thirty seconds before I put Mal down and hurried toward the house, where I thought Liz should be. "Liz," I called in a stage whisper. "Liz, are you okay?"

There was no answer so I hurried around the house. It was eerily quiet. "Liz!"

It all happened quickly after that. Mal barked. I turned. Patrick Damon stood in front of me with a flashlight shining in my eyes and the glint of a weapon. "Allie McMurphy," he said in a tone that sent a chill down my spine. "Snooping around my uncle's place. I have every right to shoot you," he said. "I mean, with a killer on the loose and you skulking around at midnight. Everyone would agree that I have every right to shoot first and ask questions later."

"Patrick," I squeaked, my mouth dry as dust. "I thought you were living at your rental."

"Please, why would I live there if my uncle's home is empty and I have a key?"

"Are you alone?" I asked.

"Are you?" he taunted me.

"I have Mal," I said, and picked my pup up. "We were out for her late-night walk."

"Strange that you're so far from your current home and walking around the back of my property."

"Mal was chasing a squirrel," I said.

"Sure, she was," he said, and sighed. "What did you see?"

"Nothing," I said. "Just a squirrel. I'm sure you heard Mal bark at it."

He was not lowering his gun. "We're going to have to go inside now."

"I'm not going inside."

"Yes, you are," he said, "or I will shoot you and I'll make sure the bullet goes through your dog's head first."

I hugged Mal to me, shielding her head with my hand. "Why are you doing this?"

"I don't like snoopy people," he said, and opened the door to the storm cellar under the house. "Get inside."

"Fine," I said. "But you have to know that this is technically kidnapping and you will go to jail for it."

"Only if they find your body." Patrick's tone sent a second chill down my spine. Mal growled against my chest. I stepped down into the storm shelter, uncertain of the stairs. It was dark and cold.

"There's a string about five steps in," Patrick said behind me. "It will turn on the light."

I stopped and looked over my shoulder at the man silhouetted against the night sky. The cellar doors were the kind that leaned against the house. It had once been a way for the coal man to deliver coal for the house without having to go inside and bother the occupants. It reminded me of the storm cellar Dorothy tried to get into in *The Wizard of Oz*.

"Don't even think about doing anything stupid," he said.

"If you shoot me, the neighbors will hear and come looking," I pointed out.

"The neighbors are gone for the winter," he said, and closed the doors, locking me into the pitch-darkness.

I fumbled for my phone and turned on my light. Turning around toward the basement, Mal barked. A shadow rushed me from my periphery and everything went dark.

Chapter 16

I dreamt of Papa Liam. He was sitting in his favorite chair, smiling at me and telling me he was proud of what I had accomplished. I told him about Frances and Douglas and my latest fudge flavor.

"Allie," he said.

"Yes?"

"Wake up!"

I opened my eyes. It was dark and I was lying on the floor. Cold seeped in through my parka, making me shiver. I tried to sit up and found my hands and ankles were bound. Mal whined softly nearby. My head hurt something fierce. It took me a moment to realize I was in the basement of the old Victorian cottage. Mal was inside an old crate. The lid appeared to be nailed shut.

The last thing I remembered was Patrick shutting the door on me. That meant whoever hit me was already in the basement. Patrick had an accomplice—or he was the accomplice. My hands were tied with a rope behind me and, from what I could make out, the rope binding my ankles was knotted neatly. Whoever tied me was familiar with nautical knots. I tried to pull my hands free, but all it did was chafe my wrists. As my eyes acclimatized to the dark, I realized it must be daylight out. Light shone weakly through the tiny cracks in the cellar doors. I made out the shape of a shovel a few feet away and scooted toward it. My heart pounded. I could probably call out, but then my captors would know I was awake. No, I decided stealth was my best bet.

Mal whined as I moved away. "Shush, pup," I whispered. The shovel was leaning against the wall. I got close enough to nudge it. The wooden handle hit me on the head and I saw stars. Trying not to curse I wiggled until I had the metal part of the shovel close enough to work the rope against and I started sawing with all my might.

I heard footsteps above me, then voices. Whoever held me was up there and probably heard me moving about. Mal was quiet and watchful as I pulled on the rope and sawed for all I was worth. Was it loosening? The footsteps were closer and I had to abandon the shovel. I hurried out from under it and scratched my way back to where I had woken up just as the door from inside the house opened.

A woman's frame was silhouetted in the doorway and I closed my eyes and pretended to be knocked out still. Mal barked and I moaned and turned my head toward the dog, pretending not to know what was going on, but careful not to show the frayed ropes that bound my hands. The door closed and I held my breath, listening to determine if the woman was in the basement or had simply gone back to what she was doing upstairs.

I waited for what seemed forever then heard footsteps walk away from the door and continue overhead. I hurried back to the shovel. It was at a worse angle now, but I found an edge and continued to work on the ropes. After what seemed like a lifetime, the ropes pulled apart. I yanked them off and quickly began to work the knots at my feet.

There were new footsteps above me and a man and a woman began to shout. I finally got my feet free and grabbed the shovel and ran to stand in the shadows of the stairwell. The footsteps were solid and full of purpose above me. The door banged open and the light came on, blinding me momentarily.

I held my breath as someone came running down the steps. I saw the glint of a gun and whacked it with the shovel. The gun skittered along the basement floor and I raised the shovel again. A familiar voice cursed low and deep. "Police, freeze!"

I stopped with the shovel in midswing as my brain realized it was Rex on the stairs and Charles at the top of the stairs.

"Allie, it's okay. You're safe!" Charles said, and turned on the basement light.

I blinked against the glare as Rex took the shovel from my hands. "It's okay. We got them." I leaned into Rex and closed my eyes. My head pounded.

Mal barked joyously from the wooden crate. Officer Brown went over to her, put his gun in the holster, grabbed a wedge, and pulled the top off the crate. Mal bounded out, licking his face. He picked her up.

"Is she hurt?" I asked as I opened my eyes. Rex had his arms around me and I didn't want to move. Even if we both had coats on. I savored the scent of his cologne.

"She's fine," Charles said, and brought her to me. "Aren't you, boo-boo?" Mal licked his face and then reached out to me and I took her in my arms.

"Come on," Rex said. "Let's get you upstairs so George can take a look at you. Charles, clear the basement and then meet us upstairs."

I walked stiffly up the stairs as Mal leaned her head against my chest and licked me under the chin. The house was filled with the bustle of a police investigation and Rex led me to a kitchen chair to sit. George, carrying his medic bag, came into the room.

"Aren't you a sight," he said as he pulled on gloves and opened his bag.

"Get her some water," Rex said to Officer Lasko, who came in behind George.

Megan Lasko winced when she saw me and hurried to the kitchen sink.

"That bad, huh?" I asked.

George gently examined the side of my head. I took a quick intake of breath at the pain his touch gave me. "Looks like you'll need a few stitches and we'll have to keep an eye on you to make sure you didn't suffer a concussion."

"I was dreaming about Papa Liam," I said as he dug into his medic bag and took out gauze, a bottle, and a syringe.

"Probably concussion," George stated. "I had one once as a kid and saw cartoon characters for hours."

"Let me take Mal," Megan said.

I reluctantly let go of my dog while George shined a light in my eyes. "What happened?" I asked as he cleaned me up. He numbed the side of my head and examined me further.

"Irma called us," Rex said. "She said she saw you and Mal leave with Liz but you didn't come back and she was worried. She thought you and Liz might have gotten into trouble sleuthing."

"Where is Liz?" I asked. "Is she okay?"

"She's fine. We found her upstairs when we found Sally Cramdon. What happened?"

"Liz and I learned that Kayla was Patrick's cousin and that she had petitioned to be included in the Ellsworth inheritance. We thought maybe Patrick had taken Sally and was hiding her here."

"That's a leap in thinking. Why did you think Patrick would hide her here?"

"The property is next to the park. It would have been easy to get Sally out the back of her cabin and into this place without being seen."

"So, instead of telling me, you came to check it out?"

My head throbbed and I struggled to keep my eyes open. "We needed proof before we bothered you with our theory."

"But Patrick found you, threatened you with a gun, and locked you in the basement."

"Yes, but there was someone already down there," I said. "They hit me and tied me up."

"Judith Schmidt," Rex said.

I winced as the numbing shot George gave me

stung my skin. "Mrs. Schmidt? What does she have to do with all this?"

"We'll talk later," Rex said. "I need to get a statement from you."

"Wait." I held up my hands and noticed the rope burns around my wrists. "Is Liz all right?"

"Yes," Rex said.

"Did you say you found Sally?"

"Yes. Now be still and let George do his job."

My thoughts whirled as George stitched me up.

"You get yourself into too much trouble," he said simply. "You need to stop and think about the people who care about you. You nearly gave Frances a heart attack."

"Wait, is Frances okay?"

"She's fine," he said, and put salve on my wrists and bandaged them. "Everyone is fine."

Outside the air was crisp and the sky so blue it hurt my eyes. The police had roped off the driveway and a crowd had gathered on the other side. I held Mal as Officer Brown helped me down the porch steps and toward the crowd.

"Allie!" Frances broke through the crowd and gave me a hug. Liz wasn't far behind. "Are you all right?"

"She's going to be fine," Officer Brown said. "I need to take her and Liz down to the station to get their statements."

"I'm going with them," Frances said, and linked her arm with mine.

"Are you okay?" Liz asked, and took my other arm.

"Sure," I said, not at all certain I was telling the truth. Mal barked and snuggled in my arms as if to say she was going to the station with me.

"Let's not discuss anything until I get both of your stories," Officer Brown said softly.

The crowd was full of people I knew. Each congratulated me for solving the case. The ladies' group grinned at me, while Mr. Beecher and some of the older men nodded at me. Harry winked at me.

"Nice look," he said.

"Douglas," Frances said. "Please take Mal and get her some breakfast."

He nodded and took Mal from me and worked his way through the crowd. Officer Brown bundled me and Frances and Liz into a carriage and took us to the administration building. My head pounded and I closed my eyes against the sway of the carriage and the sound of the horses' shoes on the cold pavement.

Frances patted my hand.

I opened one eye and looked at Liz. "What happened? Are you okay? When did you get caught?"

"Ladies, please," Charles said. "Save it for after we get your stories."

She shrugged. "I'm a good reporter. I try not to sell my story before it's printed."

I wanted to laugh at the absurdity of that statement, but it hurt too much.

Once inside the police station, I traded my coat for a thick blanket and a cup of hot coffee. I was once again inside an interview room.

The door opened softly and Rex entered. "How are you feeling?"

"Like I've been hit by a bus."

"Marron said you had to have twelve stitches," Rex said, and pulled out a chair opposite me.

I winced at the sound of the chair scraping against the floor.

"Tell me exactly what happened," he said softly. "Don't leave anything out."

"Where should I start?"

"Let's start with what happened after you left Frances."

I went through the story and tried to ignore the tic in his jaw as I told him about the ladies coming over. About how Liz and I did some digging. About why we went to the Ellsworth cottage at midnight. How Patrick forced me into the cellar and what I did when I woke up.

There was a long pause as Rex took it all in. He took a deep breath and blew it out. "Allie, why didn't you call me?"

"When?" I asked. "You were looking into Sally's apparent abduction. All we had was a theory and no proof. You would have told us to go home."

"Yes, I would have."

"So what would be the point of calling you? I mean, you couldn't check out Patrick without more evidence."

"You have to stop being a vigilante."

"I'm not a vigilante," I said. Then I put my hand on my head. "I think I'm going to be sick."

He rushed to his feet and grabbed a waste can. I emptied my stomach.

"Okay," he said. "You probably do have a concussion. Let's get you to the clinic."

"I hate the clinic," I said as he helped me to my feet. My body shook and my knees felt weak. He picked me up in his arms and carried me out. "Take me home."

"Stubborn woman. You need someone to keep an eye on you. We're going to the clinic."

It was Tuesday before I was able to go home. No one had told me anything more. Rex had my phone and there was no television in the clinic. I slept off and on and chatted with the nurses. Frances sat beside me until I sent her home. Rex came and went over my story again. Then the doctor declared me well enough to leave the clinic and Frances took me home.

Mal and Mella were happy to see me.

"Take a shower and change," Frances said. "I'll make you some scrambled eggs and toast."

"Sounds divine," I said.

Twenty minutes later I was clean and ensconced on the couch, pets snuggled up to me as I ate eggs and toast and sipped coffee. "Tell me what happened," I demanded. "How is Judith Schmidt involved in all this?"

"Judith was Patrick's mother's best friend," Frances said. "She practically raised Patrick. They grew closer after his mom died."

"Patrick didn't tell me he lost his mom."

"Yes, it was a bad stroke that took her quickly," Frances said. "It happened almost two years ago."

"So Patrick lost his uncle and his mother within the span of two years," I said.

"Yes, and just when he thought the courts were going to award him his uncle's property, Kayla came out of the woodwork. She knocked on his door asking how they could be related. Patrick was excited about the idea of family, but then Kayla hired a private investigator and when she learned how much the family fortune was worth, she hired a lawyer to petition that the Ellsworth place go to her."

"So Patrick poisoned her?"

"No," Frances said. "It was Judith who poisoned her."

"But both Patrick and Judith helped me try to save her. They did CPR on her."

"Judith knew the type of poison she gave her would still kill Kayla, CPR or not. And this way no one suspected her."

"I know I didn't suspect her," I said. "She came with my ladies to talk about the investigation and the poison. She listened while we speculated how the killer got the poison in the fudge. Wait—Sally wasn't poisoned, was she?"

"No," Frances said, and patted my hand. "Sally is fine. She was going through Kayla's stuff and discovered her daughter's petition. Sally went to Patrick that afternoon to tell him she didn't want to have anything to do with his family or their money. She was going to drop the suit."

"So why kidnap her?" I asked. "If she dropped the suit, Patrick would have gotten the money and no one would have been the wiser."

"Judith didn't believe her. She told Patrick the only way to be free of Sally's claim was to get rid of her."

"But they couldn't poison her?"

"No, Judith knew people were looking for a poisoner. She talked Patrick into taking Sally to the Ellsworth house. The plan was to murder Sally and leave a note to make it look like Sally killed herself due to the grief of losing her daughter."

"But why call you?" I asked. "I mean, if Patrick hadn't called you we wouldn't have been out looking for Sally until she was missing for a few days."

"Patrick couldn't do it. Sally is his only remaining relative. So he brought her to the Ellsworth house as Judith asked and then called me, hoping we would find Sally before Judith killed her."

"He found me and forced me into the basement," I said.

"Where Judith hit you over the head and tied you up."

"It's all still confusing. What happened to Liz? She was with me and then we couldn't find her."

"Liz had snuck into the house through an open window. She didn't know they had you and Mal. They were keeping Sally in the attic and Liz found her. She was attempting to free Sally."

"But she was discovered?" I surmised.

"Yes," Frances said. "Once they tied you up, they got into a fight. Judith felt that things were falling apart and she decided they had to move Sally because you were snooping around. They went to the attic to get Sally—they were going to push her off Lovers' Leap—but Liz got in the way."

"Oh no, they were going to make Sally jump?" I put my hand to my mouth at the thought. It was called Lovers' Leap because the cliff was tall and jutted out over rocks below and legend had it that a pair of lovers had killed themselves there when their families refused to let them marry.

"After finding Liz, they knew they couldn't get away with making Sally's death look like suicide. They argued. Patrick said Judith had gone too far. It was too much to kill you and Liz and Sally," Frances said. "They were in a panic and had forgotten to search Liz. She managed to get her phone out and called nine-one-one."

"Rex and his men stormed the house. Patrick gave himself up easily, but Judith tried to escape and was shot in the shoulder. They flew her to Cheboygan for surgery and are keeping an eye on her."

"Why did Judith poison Manfred?" I asked. "What was the connection?"

"Manfred was simply in the wrong place at the wrong time. Judith wanted to frame Frances for Kayla's murder."

"And the only connection between Kayla and Manfred was Frances."

"Yes."

"And Judith confessed?"

"No, but they found the poison in her basement. She had three more boxes of poison-laced fudge."

"She has to be insane," I said sadly.

"Patrick seemed relieved that Rex and Charles caught them before Sally was killed. He told them everything."

"And Judith?"

"As far as I know, she's recovering, but hasn't said a word, not even to ask for a lawyer," Frances said.

There was a knock on the door. Frances got up and answered it.

"Hey, girl, how are you doing?" Liz asked as she entered.

"Not bad," I said, and touched my bandaged head. "Just a little worse for wear. How are you? Any stitches?"

"No, I didn't let them sneak up on me," she said with a grin. "Still, it makes a great story. Doesn't it?" She handed me a paper with a picture of Rex with a handcuffed Patrick. "I heard you clobbered Rex with a shovel."

"In my defense, it was dark and all I saw was a man with a gun."

Liz laughed and sat down beside me. "You missed the way Rex and Charles stormed in like a cop show on television. Quite dramatic. Patrick gave up right away. I doubt he would have hurt anyone. As for Judith, she's still not talking."

"What a mess," I said. "All because a girl wanted to find her roots."

"The good news is that all the inspections passed on the McMurphy," Frances said. "Douglas started making up the rooms today. We can open for the Christmas season as soon as you're ready."

"Now, that is wonderful!" I said. "I'm looking forward to getting things back to normal."

"Oh, and I hope you don't mind," Liz said, and opened the pocket doors to the den. "But a few of us got together and decorated your Christmas tree." There in the center of the front window was the tree, where I had left it. The branches had fallen beautifully into place. It was decorated in vintage fudge shop with pink-and-white-striped ribbon to match the interior of the McMurphy lobby and twinkle lights to give it a soft glow.

"Oh, it's lovely," I said. "Thank you!"

"Douglas put the other tree up in the lobby of the McMurphy. We thought we would wait until tomorrow so that you can decorate it with us," Frances said.

"I'm so excited," I said, sitting up. "I can start making fudge in the kitchen again and I can be moved back into the apartment this weekend. It will be so nice to get back to the Christmas season."

"I bet my book club ladies will miss you, though," Frances said with a wink. "They enjoy your cookie and cheese plates."

"I'm sure now that you are no longer a murder suspect, you will go back to meeting with the girls," I said. "I'll have moved out, but as long as you don't have a renter, I don't see any reason they can't meet here."

Frances laughed. "I'm sure Irma and Barbara will love that idea."

White Chocolate Fruitcake Fudge

1 16-ounce tub cream cheese frosting
1 12-ounce package white chocolate chips
¼ teaspoon salt
½ teaspoon rum extract
1 cup mixed candied fruit
½ cup chopped pecans

Prepare an 8 x 8-inch pan by lining with foil and buttering foil.

In a microwaveable bowl, mix the frosting and white chocolate chips. Microwave on high for 1 minute. Stir until smooth. (Repeat if necessary in 30-second intervals until smooth.) Add the salt, rum extract, candied fruit, and pecans. Pour into pan. Chill until set. Cut into 1-inch pieces and enjoy! Store in airtight container.

Note: For an extra kick, soak candied fruit in rum overnight. Drain and use as above.

Makes 64 pieces of fudge.

Chapter 17

"Wow, that's some bump on your head," Harry said as he passed me in front of Doud's Market. "I heard you were an intrepid sleuth, but I had no idea you were willing to sacrifice life and limb."

"A girl's gotta do what a girl's gotta do," I said with a smile. "How's your remodel coming?"

"Slow," he said. "My worker is a bit lazy and distracted."

"Really?" I felt concerned. "Who do you have doing it? I can recommend some great guys."

He laughed, his eyes sparkling. "I can't really fire the guy."

"Why not?"

"I'm doing the work myself, remember?" He winked. "That said, I wanted to let you know I'm leaving the island for a few months. I've got some business to attend to in Florida. I would love to see you again when I get back."

"Hmmm," I said. "A lot of things change in a few months. I might be deeply involved with someone else by then. You know, have a kid or two and be settled down."

He put his hand over his heart and staggered back. "That would be horrible. I would prefer you pined away, waiting for my return." He sobered. "Can I call and text?"

"I suppose you do have my number," I said. "I promise not to block you."

"Done deal. Merry Christmas, Allie," he said, and grabbed me and kissed my cheek. "I'm looking forward to seeing you again soon."

"Merry Christmas, Harry," I said, and a warm feeling of hope entered me as I watched his gorgeous body stride down the street.

"Hey, girl."

I looked up to see my best friend, Jenn, and squealed, "Jenn! When did you get back from Chicago?" I squeezed her and then pushed her away. "You look gorgeous. Where did you get that coat?"

She smiled at me and did a little turn. "In a boutique off Michigan Avenue. Got the boots there, too." She had on jeans and a pair of brown thigh-high boots with square heels. "Is it okay that I came for Christmas? I saw the Santa Fun Run event and I just had to come."

"Sure, I've moved back into the McMurphy so your bedroom is all new and bright. Wait until you see the changes I made." I put my arm through hers. She pulled her wheeled suitcase behind her as we walked to the McMurphy. "How's Chicago? How is it that you can take these two weeks off? Aren't you swamped with party planning?"

"I hadn't heard from you in weeks and I was afraid you were mad at me for deserting you."

"I'm not mad," I said. "How can I be mad? It's Christmas and you went to pursue your dreams."

"I think my dreams are right here," she said sincerely. "Have you seen Shane lately?"

"A couple of times," I said. "How are you two getting along? I know he went down to visit you last fall."

Jenn bit her lip. "I think I messed that up, too. He hasn't talked to me in over a month."

"Well"—I patted her arm—"now that you are here, we're going to fix that right up." I pushed open the door to the McMurphy. "Oh, and I'm going to put you straight to work. I need help with the Christmas decorations. I've got a lot of stuff but I'm just not sure the best way to decorate."

"It would be my pleasure," she said.

"Jenn!" Frances came around the front desk and gave Jenn a hug. Mal came tearing over and slid into Jenn. She laughed and picked up the pup. "Hello, you guys. Gosh, how I missed this."

Douglas came down the stairs. "Well, if it isn't the prodigal friend. Hi, Jenn. Welcome back." He gave her a quick hug.

"Jenn's going to stay through Christmas," I said.

"Perfect," Frances said. "We have a full house and can use the extra hands. Go on up and get your things put up." She waved us both to the stairs.

"Wait until you see how I've redone it," I said. We reached the fourth floor and I opened the door to the apartment. It had light wood floors throughout with dark cabinets in the kitchen. "Is that granite?"

she asked as she dropped her suitcase and went to caress my countertop.

"It's PaperStone, great for hot sugar and the environment," I said.

"And stainless steel appliances." She looked impressed.

"With soft-close drawers." I pulled out a drawer and went to close it. It slowed and softly closed on its own.

"Wow," she said. "And look at the decor. So clean and modern and feminine."

I hugged my waist. "I love it, but I do miss Papa's chair."

"Please, you hated that old thing," she said.

"Yes, but I miss Papa."

"It's okay," she said. "I'm sure he's here in spirit." She put her arm through mine. "So his chair is also here in spirit. The best place for it, really. Show me my room and the bathroom."

We both laughed. She loved the spare room and the bathroom and my room. So many changes. I sat while she unpacked and we talked about Chicago and Mackinac Island. I told her about Rex and Melonie. She talked about how much she missed Shane.

"Oh, and I have so many ideas for Christmas decorations," she said. "I can't wait to get started."

"Jenn," I said.

"Yeah?"

"Thanks for coming back. You are the best Christmas present ever."

"I'm glad to be back," she said with a soft smile,

and gave me a hug. "I'm so glad you'll have me back. I promise never to leave you again."

"Let's not make promises we can't keep," I said, and hugged her back. "I'm glad you are back. Let's make this the best Christmas ever."

"A fudgy little Christmas," Jenn said, and put her arm through mine. "Now, let's see what mischief we can get into."

ACKNOWLEDGMENTS

Special thanks to everyone who made this book possible, from my agent, Paige Wheeler, to my editor, Michaela Hamilton, and all the hardworking folks at Kensington Publishing. I'd also like to the thank the staff at The Island Bookstore on Mackinac Island for their support. Finally, for all the Christmas lovers out there, I hope you enjoy this book. Cheers!

Don't miss the next delightful Candy-Coated Mystery
from NANCY COCO

Here Comes the Fudge

Coming soon from Kensington Publishing Corp.

Keep reading to enjoy a sample excerpt . . .

Chapter 1

"It's bad luck to walk under a ladder."

I stopped short and looked up to see Peter Ramfield salute me with a paintbrush. Waving back at him, I stepped off the sidewalk in front of the McMurphy Hotel and Fudge Shop to get a view of the new color. "Is it bad luck for you or me?" I asked.

"I think it's best if we don't find out either way," he said.

"Probably true," I called up. Lately I had had my fair share of bad luck and didn't want to cause it for anyone else.

At least now the McMurphy was remodeled and back to its glory. The historic committee had agreed I could go back to the original butter yellow color with pale blue trim. The old girl looked quite lovely decked out in her new colors.

"How's it looking?" Stan Hangleford called from his place on the scaffold beside Peter.

"Looks great!" I said, and did a thumbs-up motion. Stan's company had won the bid to paint the exterior of the building.

Winter retreated slowly on the island and this spring had been cold. The temperatures were only now reasonable for outdoor painting. The guys were pros, painting quickly enough to take advantage of the warmth and make the McMurphy whole again.

It was late May on Mackinac Island and we were far enough north to still get frost. I wore a spring jacket over a hooded sweatshirt and a turtleneck made of cotton and sprigged with flowers. The wind was cold off the lake and a few stubborn piles of snow dotted the shaded areas of Main Street.

But it was warm enough to paint. That's what I told myself, anyway. The early-bird pricing was also attractive.

Technically we had one week until the tourist season started. Main Street officially opened to tourists the first week of June, but I had chosen to be open year-round. During the dark, deep winter months of January, February, and March, I had only one, maybe two, guests a week. Often they were contractors working on the interiors of the stately Victorian cottages. The homes were called cottages and considered vacation homes, even though they were huge, sometimes three-story places with gingerbread accents and wraparound porches.

"Hold the door!" My best friend, Jenn, called as I went to open it. She hurried around the scaffolding. "Thanks! Isn't it gorgeous out?"

"Yes," I said. "I'm so glad spring is finally warming up—especially with the summer season starting next week." We both walked into the McMurphy's lobby. My bichon-poodle pup, Mal, greeted us with a joyous bark followed by a run and slide. She loved sliding and hitting me headfirst.

Reaching down, I picked her up and scratched her behind the ears. Mella, my calico cat, opened one eye and gave the dog a disapproving look from her curled-up position on top of one of the wing-backed chairs near the fireplace.

"I've got the most amazing good news," Jenn said. "I booked the Wilkins wedding." Jenn was not only my best friend but also a business partner, building her event-planning operation out of my office.

"Wonderful," I said. "When is it?"

"They want to be married in four weeks," she said as she opened an app on her cell phone.

"Wait, isn't your wedding in two weeks?" I had to point out the obvious. "How are you going to have time to plan hers and yours? What about your honeymoon?"

"The Wilkins wedding is the event of the year and I am not turning down the opportunity to build my brand. Besides, they want to use your new rooftop deck. Think of the view and the pictures. It'll be the best publicity of the year. People will start booking the entire hotel for the wedding party. You're only a carriage ride away from historic St. Anne's Church and the beach."

"But your wedding is a once-in-a-lifetime event," I said. "You should be concentrating on that."

"That's what I have you for," she said with a wave of her pink manicured hand. The two-carat princess-cut diamond on her finger sparkled in the light.

"I'm your maid of honor, so it's my responsibility

to let you know that I don't want work to overshadow your big day." We walked through the pink-and-white-striped lobby of the McMurphy to the back corner where the reception desk was.

Frances Devaney, my general manager for the hotel, sat behind the desk working on her computer. "I have to agree with Allie," Frances said. "As a new bride myself, I can tell you that your wedding day is more stressful than you think. Seriously, it's very different from planning someone else's."

"Pooh," Jenn said. "I have everything about my day under control." She raised her hand. "My dress is coming in this week from Chicago and I have an appointment with Annie Flannigan for final alterations. Sandy is making the cake, which is salted honey, orange blossom cake with honey and orange buttercream. She is going to make a chocolate carriage with a bride and groom figure for the top. Then the rest will be decorated with real flowers that mimic my bouquet, which I have ordered already. Terra Reeves is going to cater the reception, which will be set on your rooftop deck and set up as an informal buffet. We're having ham and scalloped potatoes, which are Shane's favorites. Bruce Miller will deejay and we'll dance the night away with family and friends."

I shook my head and smiled at the dreamy determined look on her face. "You know as well as I do that even the best-planned events can take wrong turns along the way."

"Pish," she said, and leaned on the reception desk. "I have backup plans for my backup plans. It'll be perfect and I'll have plenty of time to work on the wedding of the year."

"Where are you two going for your honeymoon?" Frances asked. Frances was seventy-three years old and had gotten married last summer to my handyman, Douglas Devaney. The two had delayed their honeymoon until after the tourist season. "The Bahamas are great. Quite a bit more sun and warmth than here, although I do love our beaches."

Frances was five feet four at one time and had shrunk an inch or two as she aged. She had short brown hair and wide brown eyes. Today she wore a long, red sweater over a yellow blouse and a yellow and red skirt that covered her knees. Her makeup was always perfectly done. I had seen pictures of her in the '60s and her hair had been a short bouffant. It still was well styled and you would guess she was in her early sixties.

"Shane and I are meeting for dinner at six to make our final choice," Jenn said. "I want to see Paris in the springtime. He's more practical and thinks we should go to Quebec instead." She sighed.

"Quebec is lovely in the spring," Frances said. "You can save money for a house."

"Oh, we don't have to save," Jenn said. "That's where I went this morning. We bought the old Carver cottage near Turtle Park."

"You bought a house?" I asked. "How did you swing that?"

"The Carver cottage has been abandoned for a decade at least," Frances said. "I heard it was on the auction block."

"Yes," Jenn said. "We got it for ten grand. It needs a new roof, new windows, new floors, and upgrades, but Shane and I are excited about doing a lot of the work ourselves."

"I didn't know Shane was into construction," I said. Shane Anderson was the crime scene investigator for Mackinac Island and St. Ignace, which was a ferry ride away on the Upper Peninsula of Michigan. Shane was also a tall, skinny man with geekish dark-rimmed glasses glasses and a warm smile.

"He put himself through college roofing homes," Jenn said. "I'm going to do the decorating. What we can't do ourselves will be done by Shane's friends."

"Sounds like fun," I said. "But are you sure you aren't doing too much?"

"Have you ever known me not to accomplish what I set out to do?" Jenn asked.

"No," I said with a smile. "But you've never been the bride before, either." I put Mal down so she could settle into her dog bed, which was beside Frances. "Just don't be afraid to ask for help. You have friends who are willing to pitch in."

"I know," Jenn said. "That's why I love you guys. Okay, I've got to scoot. I promised to set up cake tasting for Jessica Booth. She and her fiancé, Max Wilkins, and the families are all in Chicago. Good thing I know some great cake shops in Chicago."

"Wait, the Wilkinses aren't local?" I asked.

"No, silly, that's why we're going to rent the entire McMurphy for the wedding weekend."

"But don't you want to be there for the cake tasting?" I asked.

"That's why we have airplanes," Jenn said. "Which reminds me, I have to call Sophie to schedule flights up and back for myself and the family. Got to run!" She hurried up the stairs behind the reception desk.

The McMurphy's lobby took up the entire first floor of the building. At the front of the building in the right-hand corner was the fudge shop. I had walled it off in glass so that guests could watch the fudge making and my pets would be safely outside the kitchen.

Across from the fudge shop was a small cozy sitting area with free Wi-Fi, a fireplace, and open views to Main Street. Behind the sitting area was Frances's station, which included the reception desk and mailbox cubbies for the guest rooms. Across from that was another seating area with winged-back chairs, two comfy couches, and the all-day coffee bar.

Finally, there were two sweeping staircases to the upper floors and in the center of the back wall was an old-fashioned open elevator for guests who couldn't walk up the stairs.

"That girl has too much energy," Frances said with a shake of her head. "But it's great that she is going to fill the McMurphy with wedding guests."

"I know four weeks out is nearly July but it's been so cold this year. I hope it's not too chilly for the reception on the rooftop deck."

"We have the tower heaters," Frances pointed out.

"That was a good investment, by the way. Along with the white tent top."

"Those were for Jenn's reception," I said. "But if she keeps reserving the rooftop for her events, they will pay for themselves by the end of the season."

"I don't know where she gets her energy, but I'm glad she's back."

"Me, too," I said. "Her time in Chicago nearly broke my heart."

"I think we might have Shane to thank for that." Frances looked down through her brown cat-eyed glasses at her computer screen.

I agreed. Last fall Jenn had an opportunity to work for one of the most prestigious event planners in Chicago and we had all let her go. But by Christmas, Jenn had missed us and realized she couldn't be away from Shane. So she had come back and proposed her own event-planning business to be run out of the McMurphy. I had agreed immediately, of course. Shane, on the other hand, had taken his time to welcome her back. But when he did, he did it with an engagement ring.

The dead of winter isn't the best time to start an event-planning business on Mackinac Island as it's really isolated, so Jenn had gone back to Chicago until April to finish out her contract. It was great to see her so happy—even if she was making me wear a mint green bridesmaid's dress.

It was nearly nine p.m. and I was getting ready for bed when my phone blew up with a flurry of text messages. I heard the *whoosh-beep, whoosh-beep, whoosh-beep* as the messages came through. It was not a good sound. I put down my hairbrush and picked up the phone, but before I could read the messages, the phone rang. It was Jenn.

"Jenn, what's going on?" I sat down on the edge of my bed. Mal looked up at me from the floor while Mella leapt onto the bed and eased over to me.

"Shane didn't show up for dinner," she said. Her tone was one part angry and another part worried. "I sent him text messages, but he didn't answer. I called and it went to his voice mail."

"Where are you?"

"I'm in front of the Golden Goose Bar and Grill," she said. "We were supposed to meet here at seven. I waited until eight to call him. I mean, sometimes he can get caught up in his work at the lab. But he's never been this late."

"Did you call his office?"

"Yes," she said, and blew out a long breath. "He left at five. The ferry company says he was on the five-thirty ferry. So he's here, but I don't know where. I'm worried."

"I'll get dressed and meet you down there," I said. "Call Rex and see if he might know what's going on. I'll text you his cell number so you don't have to go through the police dispatch."

"Thanks," Jenn said. "I'm sorry. I know you like to go to bed early."

"Don't worry, just stay where you are and I'll meet you."

I pulled on a pair of jeans and a thick, long

pullover sweater. Mal followed me around, her stump tail wagging hard. "Oh, you think you're going out?"

She was totally going out with me. When it came to my friends and my fur babies, I would drop everything to make them happy. I put on her halter and leash. She grabbed her leash with her mouth and followed me out of the apartment, down the stairs, and out through the lobby.

Luckily I remembered to snag my jacket on the way out of the lobby. We stepped outside and a brisk wind rushed off the lake, forcing me to zip my coat quickly and pull my gloves out of my pockets. Mal followed along beside me, carrying her leash. We were a block away from the bar when Mal spotted Jenn and sprinted toward her.

"Mal!" Jenn called her name and picked her up and scratched her behind the ears.

"I thought you could use a couple of friendly faces," I said. "Did Rex know anything?"

"No," Jenn said, and I could see the dark shadows of worry on her face from the light given off by the bar. "He said it had only been a couple hours and he was certain there was nothing to worry about."

"But you're worried," I said.

"Shane's never done this," she said. "Never. And then to not pick up my calls or even send me a text . . . something is wrong."

"I agree," I said, and put my arm through hers. "But it's freezing out here. Let's go grab a coffee at the Lucky Bean and make a plan."

"Okay," Jenn said, and sounded a little bit comforted by my and Mal's presence. "I'm glad you came. I didn't know what to do. I couldn't just go home and wait. What if he's lying in a street somewhere, hurt?"

I gently guided her toward Market Street and the Lucky Bean, which was across from the police station. She clung to Mal like a lifeline. My pup loved the attention and I was glad I had brought her. "I know Rex downplayed your concern, but don't think he's not looking for Shane, too."

The streets were dark and lit by a handful of replica gas lights that now burned electricity. A horse-drawn carriage went by, the hooves clipping at a slow, steady state. Mackinac Island banned all motor vehicles except for the fire truck, ambulance, and plow. It meant that most people got around by horse-drawn carriages, bicycle, or walking. I liked the fact that life moved at a slower pace here. It drew people to vacation on the island and enjoy a step back in time.

We got to the mouth of the alley that ran between Main and Market streets. Mal sniffed the air, barked, and leapt out of Jenn's arms.

"Mal!" we both called at the same time as she took off, dragging her leash down the alley away from the McMurphy. We hurried after her. The alley was dark and filled with trash bins and back-door decks of the apartments and shops that lined Main Street.

"I can't see her," Jenn said.

I pulled out my phone and hit the flashlight app. It lit a few feet in front of us. I heard Mal bark. We moved swiftly in her direction. Mal stopped and barked again. My flashlight caught the shadow of a man wearing a short coat. His back was to us and when he turned we recognized him.

"Shane!" Jenn and I said at the same time.

Shane turned and the light from my phone glinted off metal in his hand. Something dark dripped from what looked like a hunting knife. I stopped cold when I saw a heap at Shane's feet.

"Shane?" Jenn slowed as her brain registered the scene.

"Call nine-one-one," Shane said. His voice sounded shaky. "There's been a murder."

Connect with Us

Visit us online at
KensingtonBooks.com
to read more from your favorite authors, see books
by series, view reading group guides, and more.

Join us on social media

for sneak peeks, chances to win books and prize packs,
and to share your thoughts with other readers.

facebook.com/kensingtonpublishing
twitter.com/kensingtonbooks

Tell us what you think!

To share your thoughts, submit a review,
or sign up for our eNewsletters, please visit:
KensingtonBooks.com/TellUs.